THE TRUTH ABOUT ME

The Truth About Me

Stories

Louise Marburg

wtaw press

Direct all inquiries to:
Editorial Office
WTAW Press
P.O. Box 2825
Santa Rosa, CA 95405
www.wtawpress.org

Cover Art *Neighbors #4* © by Arne Svenson
Author photo by Sandi Feldman

WTAW Books are printed in the United States of America
on acid-free paper.

Library of Congress Control Number: 2017936403
ISBN: 978-0-9988014-0-7

For Charlie

Contents

THE TRUTH ABOUT ME

THE FRONT HALL OF MY NEW HOUSE was crowded with junk: soggy cardboard boxes; an old bamboo cage; an armless coat rack, a chest of drawers with no drawers; and a heap of worn-out but elegant shoes, the discards of a fashionable woman. I didn't know who had lived there before—I bought the house from a bank—but whoever they were, they'd moved away long ago, because the place was derelict and needed repairs both obvious and as yet undiscovered.

My house was in an area we called "Sewage" when I was a kid, but was properly known as Seward, the kind of neighborhood where people sat on their stoops in the summertime and left their Christmas lights up all year long. In affluent Llewellyn Gardens, where I grew up, the houses had patios and people took down their lights. So the stoop-sitting and unseasonable lights were proof enough that Seward was a lowly place, and the taunt "Where are you from, Sewage?" was a common, if mild, insult of my youth. Later, when my friends and I were old enough to drive, we would go to Seward to buy beer at a package store where the guy at the register didn't ask for ID. "You going to Sewage?" was a hopeful question, then, for anyone who had the use of a car.

The package store was gone by the time I bought my house, and Seward was becoming a vaguely hip area. Students from the

Art Institute rented rooms there during the school year, and people from other neighborhoods came to eat at a local restaurant called the HiLo that served oysters and crabs.

"Gentrifier!" my neighbor accused when I went over to say hello, though as far as I knew I was the only "yupster," as he put it, to buy into the neighborhood. It was summer and he was bare-chested, a massive barrel of a man, with a fringe of hair around his head like a medieval tonsured monk. It was October before I saw him put on a shirt, and he wore knee-length, multi-pocketed shorts right up until Thanksgiving dinner. His wife had a job at the spice factory doing something clerical; he was on temporary disability after dropping a box on his foot while delivering packages for UPS. He told me to call him Mun, and introduced his wife as Gina. I said my name was Harry, even though I had always been called Harold. Our houses were attached to each other; I thought it was important that we get along.

"You won't be the only one for long," he said. "More will follow, and next thing you know, there'll be a Starbucks on the corner. Good Christ." He settled heavily into a rusty metal lawn chair he'd set up on the sidewalk in front of his house. "And what that means for me is higher real estate taxes." He made me tell him what I paid for my house, and was impressed by how little it cost. "But it's a piece of shit," he said. "Practically falling down. Those are asbestos shingles, you know. Gotta get rid of them safely, and it'll cost you a pantload to do it."

I didn't think that was true; I hoped it wasn't. The shingles looked like they were made of tar, with bits of mica imbedded in them that winked in the afternoon sun. My idea was to eventually replace them with white clapboard siding, fresh and clean, and to put green shutters on the front windows. I had a lot of ideas. I thought about the house all the time; I even dreamt about it. I dreamt it had a back yard, which it did not, and that the parlor had become a ballroom. The ballroom dream was particularly vivid because of the shock of the discovery. I didn't ask for a ballroom! I screamed at somebody, a stranger, who was standing in the ballroom with me. I often saw strangers in my dreams in those days. My psychiatrist said it was because of stress. I was supposed to avoid stress as if it were a food that would kill me. But buying a house wasn't even on the Holmes and Rahe scale of the top ten most stressful life events. My psychiatrist had never heard of the Holmes and Rahe scale. I'd been seeing him since I was nineteen, almost five years, and he was old, over seventy.

"Retirement is number ten on the Holmes and Rahe scale," I said.

"You should get a job before you think about retiring," he said. He thought he was being funny.

There was useless crap all over the house, not just in the front hall. Someone who'd lived there had a fondness for broken lamps, because there were maybe twenty of them in the basement, and I supposed the same person had collected the dozens of table fans and toasters and various other gadgets, all broken too, that I found in a bedroom upstairs. There were dusty cans of food and stacks of piss-yellow newspapers, and perfumes so ancient they had condensed to dark smears in their bottles. I found a laundry bag full of enough pink sponge hair curlers to set the hair of every woman on the block. On the floor of a closet off the kitchen lay two small pelts of brown and white fur with shriveled feet attached to them. I picked one up between my finger and thumb and took it over to Mun's. He was sitting in his lawn chair in the narrow shade of his house.

"Oh, yeah, that guy," he said when he saw the pelt. "I'd forgotten about him. He died, then his wife. When was that, about six years ago?"

"I don't know when," I said. "What kind of animal was this?"

Mun looked disgusted. "Guinea pig. They kept them as pets."

I dropped it on the sidewalk. Mun kicked it into the gutter.

"What's with all the broken lamps and stuff?" I said.

"Mister Fix-It," Mun said. "Pete Delarosa was his name. He died about a year after we moved in. He liked fixing stuff. Except he never did. He used to go around asking for items to repair, but people stopped giving him things when they realized they were never going to get them back."

"So he was nuts."

"Batshit. He and his wife died within a few months of each other. Someone bought the place after that, I don't know who. He never lived there, I know that. Let the house go empty when he could've rented it out. He must have been rich, like you."

"I'm not rich." I sat down on the bottom step of his stoop. The sun was right in my eyes. "If I were rich I would have hired someone to clean out the house for me instead of picking up dead guinea pigs myself."

"You got a point," Mun said. "You never told me what you do for a living."

"I'm a translator." That was what I always told people who asked what I did for a living because it was the kind of job that allowed a person to both set their own hours and work from home. Dutch was the language I chose to say I translated because I'd never met anyone who spoke it.

"Dutch! Where'd you learn that?" Mun said.

"College." If he had asked what college, I would have told him Johns Hopkins. I did go to Johns Hopkins for most of my freshman year, so it wouldn't have been a total lie. But he didn't ask. I pulled on the sweaty neck of my T-shirt and watched a couple of cars whoosh past. Some kids started shouting at each other down the street, and I heard the beeping of a truck backing up. I began to get the gelatinous feeling that always came on when I forgot to take my meds. I rarely missed taking them, and never on purpose, but I didn't feel like getting up and going inside right that minute. There was a lot to be said for sitting on a stoop. I understood now why people did it. There was an easy silence between me and Mun that I liked and wanted to continue. I wondered how old he was, and decided on thirty. Though I knew he was on disability for a hurt foot, I hadn't noticed him limping.

"Okey doke," he finally said. "Time to get us a beer."

We went up the street to the HiLo, and drank Pabst out of bottles at the bar. There wasn't anyone there at that time of day, midway between lunch and dinner, and the bartender sat at a table looking at Facebook on his phone, laughing occasionally at something he saw.

"You on Facebook?" Mun asked me.

I shook my head. If I had been on Facebook I would have had about five "friends," two of them being my parents and one of them my shrink. I had a classmate from high school who I hung out with now and then, and I kept in touch with my former roommate from Hopkins. My high school friend was a drug dealer, mostly pot, and had as much free time as I did. But I didn't do drugs—illegal ones, anyway—and he was almost always stoned, so we didn't have a ton to say to each other. My college roommate had gone on to business school and worked for a hedge fund now. The photo on his most recent Christmas card showed him with his pregnant wife and a fluffy white dog. When I knew him in college, he thought he might be gay and wanted to major in Theater. My plan had been to become an environmental attorney. I was wicked smart back then.

"You got a girlfriend?" Mun said. Again I told him no. "Because Gina thinks her cousin Aggie would like you." He picked at the label on his bottle. "Gina loves fixing people up, she wants everybody to get married. She keeps bugging me to ask you if you're interested. So I'm asking you. You don't have to answer."

I could think of plenty of reasons not to date Gina's cousin, but none that I wanted to tell Mun about. I hadn't been on a date in over five years, and hadn't had sex since my senior prom. The less you have sex, the less you crave it, I'd found, and I didn't want to revive the dead ember of my libido only to have to smother it again. I had come to fragile terms with the fact that there would be no happy ending for me. I took six pills a day, and heard a malignant voice if I didn't. Once, it ordered me to hang myself; I tried to do it, but the noose didn't hold, and I broke my kneecap when I fell to the floor. Before I bought my house, I'd lived with my parents, and moving out was a step that neither one had thought wise.

Not since bussing tables the summer after high school had I possessed the stamina to work a real job; I relied on an inheritance from my godmother, who had been childless and very kind. My greatest fear was being committed to the psych ward again, a place where no matter how fucked up I felt, or what the voice urged, everyone else seemed way crazier than I was, which is why I took my meds and avoided stress and saw my psychiatrist religiously. Mun would probably think I was joking if I told him the truth about me. Then he would realize I wasn't.

I took a swig of my beer and said, "Is she hot?"

I could see by the expression on Mun's big, lumpy face that I had said the right thing in just the right way. We clinked our bottles and drank to good-looking women. I felt like a character on TV.

"The shingles on my house are made of asbestos," I told my psychiatrist. "I have to hire a special company to remove them."

"I think you should leave the shingles where they are," he said.

"That would be like continuing to eat fatty foods after you've been told you have high cholesterol," I said. "They could give me lung disease, they're carcinogenic."

He peered at me over the steeple of his fingers. He had a leonine head of yellow-white hair. "I sincerely doubt that, Harold."

"No, really, it's been proven." I couldn't believe this was news to him; in fact, I was sure it wasn't. "I'm calling myself *Harry* now, by the way. I'm a regular guy."

"You know you'll never be that," he said. "We've gone over this before."

I woke with a bang, sucking air. I had taken a nap in preparation for my date with Gina's cousin Aggie, and the hot afternoon light that filled the room when I went to sleep had dimmed to a purplish glow. I dressed in fresh khakis and a polo, then changed to jeans and a T-shirt. In the end I decided on the khakis with a long sleeve shirt, the sleeves rolled up to my elbows. I took a Klonopin because

I was nervous. I hoped I looked handsome enough. Aggie only lived a few blocks away, but we had agreed to meet at the HiLo.

She was small and dark-haired and not quite plump, her face as round and white as a plate. She looked surprised when I walked in, though I knew Gina had described me, so she must have known more or less what I looked like: tall and thin with wavy brown hair. She told me about herself before I asked, in a precise and level voice, feeding me facts as if to get them over with, though I'd heard most of them already from Gina.

She was twenty-one and worked at the spice factory as the operation manager's secretary, a job that Gina recommended her for, but the operations manager was her mother's sister's brother-in-law, so she might have gotten the job anyway. The apartment building she lived in was owned by her uncle, who charged her a nominal rent; if not for that, she said, she would still be living with her parents. They and her younger siblings lived five blocks from her building, about the same distance, in the opposite direction, from me and Mun and Gina, so she was surrounded by family, and well-known in the neighborhood, at home wherever she went.

"Have you ever considered living somewhere else?" I asked.

She cocked her head as if listening to the sea in a shell. "Where else?"

"Anywhere. Another part of town, another city; another country, even." Too late, I realized it was a stupid question, a snobby question, and I was afraid I was going to alienate her even before we had ordered.

She shrugged. "No. You?"

"Me?" Yes, I'd considered it, I'd planned on it: I'd wanted to live in New York City after college and go to law school at Columbia. I had an urge to reach across the table and gently tug on one of her corkscrew curls, stretch it out and watch it spring back. My vision blurred for half a second, the Klonopin kicking in. I checked myself in the mirror above the bar. I looked fine, normal. I'd even shaved that day. "Never," I said. "Why would I?"

"Except you're not from here, you're from Llewellyn Gardens."

15

"But I always wanted to live in Seward."

"I don't believe that," she said mildly. Her teeth were straight except for one bottom incisor that stuck out from the others, disassociating itself. "Do you really speak Dutch?"

"Of course not, why would I do that?"

She laughed and said, "You're funny. I've never heard anyone speak Dutch. Say something."

I spoke the single phrase I knew in Dutch—"I'd like a Heineken, please"—in as guttural a voice as I could cough up.

She applauded me. "What a strange-sounding language!"

"It sounds better in writing," I joked.

She smiled at that and said, "You're different, aren't you."

"Than what?"

"I don't know. Than everyone else."

"Is that a good or bad thing?"

"Good," she said decisively.

The bartender put down our drinks.

I did reach out then and pull on a curl. "Boing," I said as I let go.

I bought cans of white paint and all manner of painting paraphernalia, brushes and rollers and sponges and trays, everything I could think of. I didn't have any decorating ideas, so painting everything white made sense for that reason, and also because I didn't know what I was doing and could be sloppy without it showing. The one thing I forgot to buy were drop cloths for the floors, so I disguised my splats and drips by painting them white as well. The rooms in the house were low and small, but as I painted they seemed to grow. I understood it was an optical illusion, but it still made me feel a little crazy.

Mun came to look at it after I'd finished.

"What the fuck?" he said. "What'd you paint the floors for? It looks like a hospital ward."

It looked nothing like a hospital ward. The rooms in hospital wards were painted different colors—yellow and greens, mostly—and the floors were usually some kind of tile. I thought the place looked wonderfully like nothing I'd seen before.

"Aggie been here yet?"

I told him she hadn't. As I didn't have any furniture but my bed upstairs, I wasn't in a position to entertain.

"She already thinks you're a weirdo," he said. "I don't know what she'll make of this."

"She thinks I'm a weirdo? Did she tell you that?"

"No. She called you *unusual*."

"Good unusual, or bad unusual?"

Mun looked at me. "You got a thing for her, huh?" He chuckled.

"What's so funny about that?"

"You and every guy in the neighborhood over the age of twelve."

I sat down on the floor, then lay down so all I could see was the ceiling. My eyes smarted against its brightness, unrelenting as sunlit snow. "I can understand that. She's beautiful. Why doesn't she have a boyfriend?"

"Picky," Mun said. "Nobody's good enough." He leaned over and looked down at me, his face framed in edgeless white.

"You think I'm good enough?" I said.

"It doesn't matter what I think," he said. "But, yeah, sure you are."

I had not had "a thing" for a girl since high school. I didn't know many girls anymore. My dead libido had come screaming back to life when Aggie had chastely kissed my cheek, and I badly wanted to have sex with her as many times as she would allow. I didn't honestly know how much I liked her because I couldn't think about anything else. Whatever she wanted, I wanted to give it to her so she would grant me this one thing in return.

I asked Mun what he thought she wanted.

"The usual stuff," he said. "Husband, house, family. She's not complicated, she's just picky. She likes you, though. She said so."

Mun must have told Gina how much I liked Aggie, and Gina must have told Aggie, because the next time we were together, she possessively tucked her arm in mine as I walked her home from

Gina and Mun's, where we had gleefully smashed crabs with wooden mallets and sucked the meat from their bodies and legs. I had never eaten crabs that way before, but now it was the only way I ever wanted to eat them. Aggie had been ruthless with her mallet and monstrously sexy all evening, so when we got to her building and she suggested I come up to her place, I almost fainted from excitement in her foyer. I don't know how long it had been since I'd had a wish come true. It was as if a butterfly had landed in my hand.

"Pink is my favorite color," she said as she unlocked her apartment door. "A lot of people think it's too much, but it's my place and I can do what I want."

"I couldn't agree more," I said, thinking of my white floors. The apartment was just one room and a little kitchen, and except for the appliances and bathroom fixtures, everything in it was pink. "Holy moly," I said, looking around. Pink carpeting, pink walls, pink sofa-bed, pink lamps, pink curtains at the windows; I felt like I had stepped inside a bottle of Pepto-Bismol.

She went into the kitchen and brought out a couple of cans of Pabst and we sat down on the sofa bed.

"This pulls out," she said.

"I figured."

"Mun and Gina are so great, aren't they?"

"They really are," I said.

"Crab is my favorite food. What's yours?"

"Crab," I said because it was all I could think of at the moment. Blueberry pie was actually my favorite. We were silent then. We drank our beers. I was so wrought up by her proximity I couldn't think of anything to say.

"Do I smell like crab?" she asked.

"I don't think so." I leaned in to smell her and she kissed me on the mouth. I followed her lead, and kissed her back, opened my mouth when I felt her tongue push against my teeth. She took my hand and put it on her breast and cupped my hard-on through my pants.

"Am I going to have to do everything?" she said. There was a lamp behind her that made me see stars. I felt her lipstick tacky on my mouth.

"No, I just didn't know how far—"

"All the way," she said.

My hands shook as I unbuttoned her shirt, and she must have noticed because it took me a long time—there were a lot of buttons and they were small. She sped things up by taking off her pants, and then mine, and dragging my T-shirt over my head. She pulled the sofa into a bed with an athletic ease that startled me.

I tried to think of other things—I counted backward, I envisioned my mother—but still I came in about thirty seconds. Her body was round and soft and white; her breasts were smaller than I'd imagined, but heavy in my hands. Her thighs were sturdy, covered in a down of dark hair. Her shoulders made me think of birds. Birds were in my head, anyway; I'd been noticing them all day. I saw two blue jays fighting in an ailanthus tree. They dipped and swirled and crashed into each other, then retreated to their separate branches before going at it again. I must have watched them for an hour. Now I saw birds wherever I looked, like learning a new word then suddenly hearing it all the time.

"You remind me of *Odalisque*," I said.

She stretched her arms over her head. "What's that?"

"A painting by Manet. He was an Impressionist artist."

"I don't know anything about art, Harry, but I'm going to take that as a compliment."

"I mean it as a compliment."

She propped herself up on her elbow. "We should do it again, don't you think?"

"Yeah. I'm sorry. That wasn't so great."

She took charge of me without embarrassment. She told me what to do and where to do it, and I followed her directions closely. Sad to say, I had never made a girl, a woman, climax before. I was busy being mentally ill during the years when I would have learned how. With stunned fascination I watched her breathe and shudder, her eyes wide as a frantic animal's. Then she closed her eyes and arched her back and cried out in a way that made me wonder if I was hurting her. I saw that she was in her own world and was briefly, sharply, jealous, but then she pulled me to her and we were together again. I was in love, but afraid to confess it.

"Will you be my girlfriend?" I said instead. Pathetic, idiotic, childish.

She looked at me for what seemed like a long time, studying my face with interest and what I interpreted as concern: people always ended up feeling sorry for me, and she wouldn't be any different. I looked around for my clothes, ready to go home.

"What, do you think I sleep around?" she said. "I already am your girlfriend."

Up until then my house had been a house; now I saw it as a home. Aggie could paint the whole thing pink if she wanted. She came over and looked around.

"I remember when Mr. Delarosa lived here," she said. "His wife was sweet. They gave out mini donuts at Halloween. Now it looks like no one ever lived here." She regarded the floors without comment. She was wearing her work clothes, a sleeveless navy dress and heels so high they must have hurt her feet. She was an hourglass silhouette. She crossed her arms and looked out the front window. "There's a blue jay in the tree out there," she said. "I don't think I've ever seen a real blue jay before."

I took this as a sign. When I was crazy, everything was a sign of something. I didn't think like that anymore. But I still believed in the occasional augur. The blue jay had not appeared by mistake.

"What you need..." she said as she walked upstairs.

I didn't hear the rest. I lay down on the floor and listened to her footsteps as she toured the rooms above, thinking I would never put down carpets so I could always hear that sound. "I love you," I said out loud a few times. My phone rang in my pocket. I had skipped my psychiatrist appointment that morning and he had been calling every few hours, but I could tell by the ring tone that this was a text. I never got texts. I rarely got phone calls. I took the phone out and read, *Please call me as soon as you see this.* During our last appointment I told him I was in love with Aggie.

"You think you're in love," he said. "But how can you be? You don't know anything about her."

"Actually, I know a lot about her," I said. "I know her relatives, I know where she works, I've stayed at her apartment; I've used her shower. Her favorite food is crab, and her favorite color is pink. Her favorite store is Banana Republic." I thought her choice of store was a classy one, given her meager salary.

"And what does she know about you?" He raised a bushy white eyebrow. "Have you told her about your illness? Do you plan to? Obviously you will have to. You must realize that."

It occurred to me that I could see a different psychiatrist if I wanted to, someone who didn't know me.

"Why are you lying on the floor?" Aggie said. She leaned against the doorjamb, dangling a shoe off one foot.

"It's nice," I said. "It's relaxing. Come join me."

"Hah, right," was all she said. "It's boiling in here. I'm going over to Gina's."

She clacked out the door and down the front steps. I could hear her heels on the sidewalk. "Hey, Mun," I heard her say. Mun said hey back. A second later, I heard the squeak of his sneakers. He came in and handed me a can of beer before cracking one of his own.

"Shit, this place is like an oven. Why do you lie on the floor all the time?"

"There's no place to sit, for one thing," I said. "But really, I like looking at the ceiling."

"Why? There's nothing up there."

"Exactly. It's like looking at nothing."

"It *is* looking at nothing."

As he sat down beside me, we heard a happy shriek from next door.

"Gina's pregnant. Sounds like she just told Aggie."

I sat up. The room spun. "Wow."

"I know, right? The circle of life." He shook his head as if trying to wake himself up. We sat there drinking our beers until I remembered what I wanted to ask him.

"How well did you know Gina when you two got married?"

"We grew up together. You knew that."

I nodded. I did, but forgot. "Do you think you have to know everything about your spouse?"

He finished the beer and crushed the can in his fist. "Sure, yeah, I think you have to know everything. If I found out Gina was keeping something from me I would be pissed. That's the whole point of being with someone, isn't it? One for all and all for one. You have to have complete trust."

All of a sudden everything seemed impossible. I felt tired just thinking about trying to act like someone else. "I'll always be alone."

"Why is that?" Mun said. He turned and really looked at me. The perspiration on his broad forehead glittered in the evening light.

"Because I'm mentally ill." I tapped the side of my head. Foolish tears of self-pity burned my eyes. "I'm crazy. I have to take medication to control it. And I'm not a translator; I don't speak Dutch. I didn't even graduate from college. I live off a small inheritance, just enough to buy this house and not have to work a job."

He scratched his chest. "I'm not surprised."

"What do you mean? What part of that doesn't surprise you?"

"I don't know. All of it. I can't say why. No, I can. First of all, why would a translator from Llewellyn Gardens buy a crappy house in Seward? Then, where are your friends? Why do you never go out? How come you take naps during the day? And you know, no offense, but you're kind of an odd duck. Like lying on the floor and staring at the ceiling, for instance. That's not something anyone normal would do."

He stood up and brushed off the seat of his pants. I thought he was going to leave. He offered his hand and pulled me up off the floor. Then he belched at length without covering his mouth. We went to the HiLo as usual.

VACATIONLAND

FROM THE BACK DECK Henry looked down the forested hill to the road below hoping to see Maisie's car returning. He was sick of listening to the child cry; sick of looking at her, of talking to and about her, bored stiff by her constant presence. Little Annabelle, his sister Maisie's daughter, was named after their maternal grandmother, whose name had actually been Anna but whose personality begged for the *belle*. The idea, he supposed, was that this Annabelle number two would grow up to be similarly delightful, but at the moment she was a snotty-nosed toddler screaming for her mother.

"Your mother is *never* coming back," he said, astonishing himself. He hadn't been mean to a child, to anyone, since his own difficult childhood, when he'd been bullied by his father and so was a bully himself. He prayed that Annabelle hadn't heard him over the racket she was making. He held his breath, horrified.

Annabelle stopped crying and stared at him, her blue eyes round as marbles, a wisp of hair glued across one wet cheek. Then she let out a shriek so piercing that Henry covered his ears with his hands. His girlfriend, Karen, came out to the deck, picked up the little girl, and held her on her hip in the way he'd seen mothers do. But Karen wasn't a mother. He was surprised by how natural she looked.

"She's hysterical!" she said. The child fought and twisted, pushing against Karen's shoulder with her chubby little hands. "What happened?"

"She wants Maisie," Henry said.

He looked to the road again. Maisie had put Henry in charge of Annabelle for "just a sec," while she ran out to the store. Annabelle's father was in the den upstairs, supposedly cooking up another blockbuster movie and fielding calls from his production company. There was never a question that Jerry might help out with his own child—or with anything else, for that matter. Henry was fairly sure his brother-in-law was up there smoking a doobie and trawling Internet porn. He was fifty-six and behaved as if he were twenty. Maisie had just turned thirty.

"Oh, baby," Karen said. "Mommy will be right back." She carried Annabelle in through the patio doors. "Where's Monkey?" Henry heard her say. "Let's have tea with Monkey." Monkey was Annabelle's favorite toy. Monkey had lost his tail last year and had to have it sewn back on; recently Monkey went missing for a day, but was thankfully found in Maisie's car. Henry knew as much about Monkey as he wanted to, but he was pretty sure there was more to come.

He leaned on the deck's railing, the sun hot on his back, and smelled the gift shop scent of pine. Maine. Vacationland. Jerry and Maisie had rented the massive glass and shingle house high over Penobscot Bay from some Hollywood associate of Jerry's, and Maisie had asked Henry to come visit them from Boston over the Fourth of July.

"And Karen, of course," she'd said a beat too late.

"Why don't you like her?"

"I do like her."

"No, you don't."

"Okay, I think she's conceited."

"You just think that because she's beautiful."

"Maybe."

"What else? Bring it on."

"I think she's tough."

"As nails," Henry said. "That's one of the things I love about her."

He watched Karen through the glass door to the living room. Kneeling at a child-size plastic table, she drank pretend tea from a tiny cup. Her braided red ponytail hung straight down her back. When it was loose, it curled like fire—he'd never seen such a color. Because she didn't ogle cute babies or pay much attention to the few kids they knew, he'd assumed she wasn't into children, but now here she was appeasing a tedious two-year-old and talking foolishness to a stuffed monkey. Maisie's car turned into the pebbled driveway.

"Mommy's home!" he happily called, breaking up the little party. As Annabelle ran out to her mother, he lit a cigarette, blew the smoke into the mossy shade of the pines, and quickly took another drag. He made himself dizzy smoking this way, but in a moment Maisie would catch him and insist he put out the cigarette. Why was it okay for Jerry to smoke weed upstairs but not okay for him to smoke a cigarette within ten feet of the house? *Because you don't make four million dollars a year*, he told himself. Jerry could do anything he wanted.

"Put that out, please." Maisie stood at the door.

"Yes, ma'am."

"Karen said Annabelle was crying for me."

The current of pleasure beneath the concern in her voice grabbed at the center of his chest. "Of course she was, Maize. You're her mom."

"Well, she seems okay. Karen has a way with kids."

"So now you like her?"

She squinted and scratched a mosquito bite on her arm, gazing out to the distant bay and the sailboats like chalk marks on the water. She wore a silvery T-shirt and a pair of white slacks. Maisie had been something of a bombshell before she got pregnant with Annabelle, with a curvaceous figure and feline eyes that she liberally played up with mascara. Now she was frankly overweight and didn't seem to care. She called her cropped haircut "sassy." Henry thought it made her look gay.

"You know I never think any of your girlfriends are good enough." She laughed at herself. "You're my little brother, I'm protective of you."

"Me too you." He and Maisie had always been each other's champions and defenders. Their father was a narcissist, their mother obsequious and timid. Growing up, they'd had an "us against them" policy that persisted like an outdated law.

Karen joined them. Tall and lithe in her shoulder-baring dress, she moved with a light-footed, sensuous ease, obviously aware of herself. She raised one long, muscled leg, rested it on the railing, bent forward and grasped her ankle.

"I gave Annabelle some grapes to snack on," she told Maisie. "She's watching *The Lion King.*"

"Grapes!" Maisie rushed into the house calling Annabelle's name, her sandals slapping the floor.

"What?" Karen said. "Is there something wrong with grapes?"

Henry knew without having to be told. "She might choke on one."

Later on Maisie left Annabelle sleeping under the supervision of the woman who cleaned the house, and they all went out for a lobster dinner. As they drove along the bay, the reflections of the setting sun bounced over the white-capped chop. Henry put on his sunglasses and watched a graceful sloop sail parallel to the shore, its jib fat with wind. He touched Karen's hand and pointed to the boat. She smiled and nodded but seemed more impressed by the big old houses on the other side, antique relics expensively preserved, with deep porches and velvety lawns.

"It's not a fancy restaurant," Maisie said. "It's not the Four Seasons. But it's not meant to be, that's the charm of it. And I hear their lobster is the best in Maine."

Henry realized that she wasn't talking to Karen or him; she was talking, obliquely, to Jerry, who was silently driving the car. He guessed that Jerry objected to Maisie's choice of restaurant because it wasn't starred in the Michelin Guide. Jerry liked everything connected to him to be, if not perfect, then outstanding, which explained Maisie's exaggerated description of the lobster.

"You like lobster, Jerry?" He was sitting directly behind the driver's seat and could see only Jerry's wide, rounded shoulders and the top of his freckled head.

"Love it." Jerry adjusted the rear view mirror so he could look at him. Henry studied Jerry's sunburned face, his potato-shaped nose and the bags beneath his eyes, and thought of the tale of the emperor without clothes. Jerry had no idea how ugly he was. "I'm not crazy about handling the things, though. A mess."

"That's why they give you a bib."

Jerry snorted. "Like I'd wear a bib."

It wasn't until the lobsters were set down on their table that Henry understood. Bibless, Jerry nursed a glass of bourbon, his lobster sitting undisturbed, while everyone else dug in. Once Maisie had cracked and picked her lobster, she put the tail and claw meat on a butter plate and exchanged it for Jerry's meal.

"What the—" Henry almost laughed.

Maisie tromped on his foot. They sat on benches at a rough plank table, and he and Maisie faced Karen and Jerry. He looked at his sister; she shook her head. He frowned into his plate. He speared his tail and claw meat, placed it on his butter plate, handed it to Maisie, and took Jerry's lobster for himself. He flagged a waitress to take the extra plates away. Readjusting his bib, he cracked a claw.

"Isn't this delicious?" he said into the silence.

"Fantastic," Karen said. "This is the first time I've had lobster! I've had every other shellfish, I think, but never lobster."

"What else haven't you had?" Jerry said. He crammed pink meat into his mouth.

"I don't know, a lot of things. Caviar, I've never had that." She pushed her hair away from her face with the back of her hand. It covered her shoulders like a brilliant shawl. "I've always thought caviar was gross."

"It's not," Jerry said. "Not the good stuff."

"Well, if I'm offered the good stuff, I might reconsider," Karen said.

"You will," Jerry said.

"Why is that?" Henry said. It would be like Jerry to have a tin of caviar in the refrigerator.

"Pretty girls attract the best things."

Henry sat back. "She just said she thinks it's gross."

Jerry looked up from his food. Butter glazed his chin. "How old are you?" he asked Karen.

"Twenty-six."

"That's how old I was when I married Jerry," Maisie said.

"Oh, wow," Karen said. "No way I'm ready for that."

"Life will surprise you," Jerry said. "You never know what you're ready for."

"Would you care to elucidate?" Henry said.

Jerry thought about it, his fork poised mid-air. "No, not really."

"Well then, thank you, Buddha," Henry said. No one spoke. "That was supposed to be funny."

"Well, it wasn't," Maisie said. Her cheeks were pink. She got up and left the table.

Henry followed her out the restaurant's door and into a cluster of trees behind the parking lot. He found her standing with her forehead against the trunk of a pine, weeping silent tears. Her sleeveless yellow dress stretched in creases across her back and hips. Even as a child she had been a quiet crier.

"Maize, Maize, I didn't mean anything!"

"How dare you," she said to the tree.

"How dare I what?" he said, baffled.

She turned around. "Don't you judge me! I have a perfectly nice life, and you don't know the first thing about it. Yes, Jerry is spoiled. So he doesn't like cracking lobster! I'm happy to do it for him!" She heaved a fresh wave of tears and put her hands over her face. "I don't *mind*."

"No, of course you don't. I don't know what I was thinking."

"You were thinking Jerry is an asshole."

That was exactly what he'd been thinking. He took Maisie's hands away from her face. "What's really going on, Maize? Are you okay? Are you well?" He looked into her swimming eyes. "*Is* Jerry an asshole?"

To his surprise, she laughed, a rasp. "No more than usual. Well, somewhat more. But he doesn't hit me, if that's what you're asking."

He looked around the darkening woods and blinked back his own sudden tears. Bats dipped and wheeled through the indigo twilight above the trees; a firefly winked, then another. The windows of the restaurant were bright, and he could hear the customers' chatter, but he and Maisie were hidden, Hansel and Gretel in the forest.

"Jesus, Maisie, that wasn't what I was asking! If not being hit by your husband is your standard of happiness—"

"He's jealous of the attention I give Annabelle. He says I've been neglecting him since I had her. It's hard taking care of both of their needs."

"Get some help, then! Or more help," he said, thinking of the housekeeper and cook and nanny she already had in Los Angeles, the maid who cleaned the rental house, and the local caterer who prepared most of their meals.

"Find someone to have sex with Jerry every goddamn night, then get up when Annabelle cries, which is usually three times before dawn? Nobody else can do those things for me, Henry." She slid down the tree to the ground and sat with her legs splayed in front of her. "I'm exhausted by both of them."

Henry sat down with her. He picked up a tiny pinecone and rolled it between his palms. There was nothing more he could say to her about Jerry; he had spoken his mind years ago. He'd begged Maisie not to marry Jerry. It was the worst fight they'd ever had. He'd accused Maisie of marrying Jerry for his money and Maisie said Henry was jealous and they'd gone at it like bitter enemies off and on for days.

It was true that he hadn't known Jerry any better then than Maisie knew Karen, but his opinion of the man hadn't changed. Jerry was self-absorbed and demanding and not nice enough to Maisie. Why she'd married a man like their father was a painful mystery to him. His own taste in women ran in the opposite direction from their mother, who'd never, as far as he knew, had an independent idea. Though the fight had been terrible, they reconciled before the ceremony, and Henry made a gracious toast. Until now, Maisie hadn't talked about her marriage. Henry's girlfriends, on the other hand, were always fair game.

"Maisie, I want to tell you something."

She sniffed. "Tell."

"I'm thinking of asking Karen to move in with me." It was almost dark, but he could make out her face well enough to see that she was neither surprised, nor happy, nor disapproving: it was as if he hadn't spoken.

"Do you want to marry her?" she said after a moment.

"You heard her say she wasn't ready for that."

"Hah. That's a lot of claptrap. Women always say that, then the next thing you know they're walking down the aisle. Have you ever heard a single woman say she was dying to get married?" The ground beneath the pine needles was damp. He shifted uncomfortably.

"I guess I haven't."

"Do you think she'll want to move in with you? You haven't been dating very long."

"I know. But we're in love."

Maisie put a finger to her lips. "Shh."

"So, you're interested in movies?" Henry heard Jerry say. Karen's response was inaudible. "Oh, don't worry, they're around here somewhere. Thick as thieves, those two. Maisie! Henry! Olly olly oxen free!"

"Let's go." Henry stood up and brushed the pine needles from the back of his jeans.

"Wait," Maisie said. "Not yet."

Jerry's SUV roared. Headlights sliced the dark. Firmly, Henry took Maisie's hand, and they walked to the car together.

Henry and Maisie were walking on the beach, Annabelle toddling between them, wearing a skirted two-piece bathing suit and a matching pink cotton sunhat. She kept squatting down to examine shells and seaweed, and the going was very slow. "Fyewooks," Annabelle said to Henry.

"What, honey?"

"She's saying fireworks," Maisie said.

"Oh, yes!" Henry said brightly. "Independence Day!"

"Idenstay," Annabelle said. Then, more clearly, "Monkey," and reached for the toy in her mother's hand.

"Try not to drop Monkey in the sand," Maisie said as she handed Monkey over. "I don't think Monkey can stand another round in the washing machine."

"Can't you buy another one?"

"You-know-who would notice and have an f-i-t. Besides, I don't know where I would get one exactly like it. It's not a goldfish, unfortunately."

Henry looked back over his shoulder at Karen sitting in a beach chair, reading a paperback. Jerry sat in another chair, leafing through a newspaper and smoking a cigar. The picnic that had been prepared for them waited in a large, old-fashioned wicker basket: French cheeses and baguettes and fruit and wine, a meal out of an Impressionist painting. He reached into the pocket of his trunks and took out a pack of cigarettes.

"Not in front of Annabelle," Maisie said.

He returned the cigarettes to his pocket. "Jerry's smoking a cigar."

"That's why we're taking a walk."

"Do you mind that he smokes weed?"

"Not as long as he does it in private." She pointed at an enormous rock that was shaped like the back of a turtle, bisected by the beach and the sea. Smaller rocks formed a jagged stairway to the top of the boulder or stone, and some kids were on their way down. "Let's go up there."

"I don't know," Henry said. He wanted to go back to Karen.

"Please? I'll let you smoke."

"No, you won't."

She laughed. "You're right, I won't."

"Watah," Annabelle said.

"No, honey, the water is too cold. Even Mommy can't go in without freezing her tush off. I wish we could, but no."

"Why Maine, then?" Henry said. "Why didn't you rent a place in Martha's Vineyard or Long Island, someplace where the ocean is warmer?"

Maisie sighed and pulled Annabelle away from the lapping waves. "Because Jerry doesn't *know* anyone who goes to the Vineyard or the Hamptons, so he doesn't think they're worth going to. He does know a few people who go to Maine, and his agent offered us the house."

"Presidents go to the Vineyard. Clinton, and I think Obama did too."

"Not presidents of movie studios. It was between Maine and Aspen, and I chose Maine because it's closer to you."

"Aw," Henry said.

"Oh, for God's sake," she said.

They climbed up the rock and sat on its warm, sandy top, Annabelle and Monkey in Maisie's lap. Below, the sea was calm, a deep oily blue. Deer Isle and North Haven were crisply visible, but Isle au Haut and Swan's Island further out were shadowed by a lace of clouds.

"Uh oh," Maisie said. "I hope those clouds blow out to sea or there won't be any fireworks tonight."

"Uh oh!" Annabelle parroted, and crawled out of Maisie's lap. Maisie went after her and held her hand as she investigated the bleached shards of shells that seagulls had dropped from above. Henry watched for a moment before turning his attention to Karen, who'd risen from her beach chair and stood by the water. She dipped in a toe, immediately hopped away, and rubbed her arms as if she were cold. Placing her fists on her hips, she leaned deeply from one side to the other, her feet planted wide in the sand. After a moment, she stretched her arms straight up and planted one foot on the opposite thigh above the knee. Tree pose. An inch of tanned buttocks peeked from her bikini bottom—under which he knew her skin was pale and soft as chamois. He felt aroused just looking at her. Her skin glistened from sunblock. A small breeze played with her hair. She lowered her hands and pressed them together as if in prayer. She went to yoga almost every day: her body was slim and muscular. She'd gotten him to go, too, and he was actually pretty good. He wanted to climb down and join her, but as he started to get up, he froze.

Jerry had spread his newspaper across his lap and was watching Karen with open-mouthed lust, one hand holding his fat black cigar and the other hidden in his crotch. Henry looked around for Maisie, but luckily she was on the other side of the rock with Annabelle, cooing over something they'd found. Karen bent over and touched her palms to the sand, then slid them forward so that she formed a triangle with the ground in a downward-facing dog. Her bikini bottom rode up to expose two slivers of white flesh. Private flesh. *Mine*, Henry thought.

Jerry took a puff of his cigar. Karen relaxed her back and fell into an upward dog. Stretching her neck, she faced the sky so that her hair fell in a bright river to her waist, then she pulled her knees forward and sat on her feet. She bent at the waist and touched her forehead to her thighs in a pose of supplication. The knuckles of her spine ran like a stairway to where the dark crack of her ass split a strip of snowy skin.

She stood up after a minute and pivoted around. Jerry's hand was still in his crotch. She smiled at him. He smiled at her. The sight took Henry's breath away.

"Annabelle, no!" Maisie called. "Henry, grab her!"

Annabelle raced past with Monkey. Henry reached out for the child but missed. He scrambled up. She was as quick as a minnow. Her hat had blown off and her downy hair flew around her head in a crazy halo. "Annabelle, *no!*" he yelled just as she disappeared off the rock. He ran to the edge and looked down at the water. Maisie screamed. He took a breath and jumped. The cold hit him like electricity.

Annabelle floated a couple of feet beneath the surface. Her skin looked green through the murk; a whip of brown seaweed was snagged on her ear. Her eyes were wide with shock. Bubbles oozed from her open mouth. Henry hooked one arm around her chest and pulled her up. Awkwardly, he paddled with his other arm and kicked toward shore as hard as he could. He'd never been much of a swimmer, and holding Annabelle's face out of the icy water and making progress toward dry ground was a challenge he wasn't sure he was up to.

Maisie ran down to the beach and waded out to meet them. Annabelle coughed and cried and puked seawater on her mother's shoulder while Maisie hugged her and wept in relief. Every fiber of Henry's body was lit with pain. His teeth chattered and his lips were frozen.

"Monkey!" Annabelle wailed. She pointed to the water.

Monkey bobbed several yards out, taken by the tide.

The fog rolled in around seven o'clock, obscuring the view from the deck. A web of mist hovered beneath the pines, and the air had grown damp and heavy. Despite several cups of tea, a shot of scotch, and an itchy pullover he'd found in an upstairs drawer, Henry still felt the cold shock of the water like a wire running through his body. He lit a cigarette and took a deep drag. Maisie was upstairs with Annabelle and wouldn't have cared, anyway. All that mattered to her now was that Annabelle was safe. For him the world had split apart. Yesterday seemed like a distant place where nothing was important. Today he had saved a life.

Tomorrow he would mourn an innocence he hadn't known he possessed. Innocence or stupidity.

"So what," Karen had shot back at him when he told her he'd seen her on the beach. *So what?* He had been knocked speechless.

"You were putting on a show for him."

"He *asked* me to, okay?" she said, looking away, avoiding his eyes. "He wanted to see me do yoga. I can't help it if he was turned on."

"Oh, come on, Karen, do you honestly believe Jerry is interested in yoga? What did you think was going on under that newspaper?"

"How should I know?" she said in a sulky tone. Then, "You left me with him, Henry," as if he should have known better.

He watched her now through the sliding door to the living room. She sat in an oversized armchair under the mellow light of a lamp, one leg beneath her and her chin on her fist, her eyes wide with interest, her mouth poised to smile. Jerry sat on the couch with a drink in his hand, wearing a fresh pink dress shirt and a pair of black jeans. His legs were spread wide, and he gestured expansively, telling a story thick with the names of celebrities, Henry knew, because that was the only kind of story Jerry told.

Karen laughed and clapped like a little girl. *The one about Bobby De Niro*, Henry thought, *the one about Tom Cruise*. She crossed her long legs and hooked a foot around her calf. Her breasts weren't big, but her blouse was unbuttoned to mid-chest so that they were visible when she leaned over. *Really? Is that all you've got?* Henry wanted to say. That she couldn't rise above being a cliché almost made him feel sorry for her. He was sorry for himself for exactly the same reason: if she was the bimbo, he was the sucker.

"Hey," Maisie said as she came out to the deck.

Henry turned around and leaned on the railing. "I thought you were with Annabelle."

"I got her to sleep," she said. She watched Jerry and Karen for a moment. "Jesus, would you look at those two?"

"I'm trying not to, but I can't help myself."

"It is kind of fascinating."

"When did you know?"

"At dinner last night."

"I just thought that was Jerry being...Jerry."

"No, that was Jerry flirting, actually. That was what really set me off, not you, but I didn't want to admit it. I still get upset when he does it in front of me."

"He does it a lot?"

"Oh, yeah. He's been screwing around with other women since Annabelle was born, and probably before then, too. He stockpiles

Viagra. He says he has to have as much sex as he can with as many women as possible before he gets too old to do it anymore. Doing it with me isn't enough, apparently."

Henry looked at her. "Seriously?"

"That's what he said."

"I'm sorry."

She shrugged. "Honestly, I don't care as much as I used to. I stopped loving him a couple of years ago. I stopped liking him more recently. But I understand what Karen sees in him. I saw it myself. Jerry is powerful, and very charming when he wants to be. He's dynamic, for lack of a better word. Oh, I know," she said when Henry grimaced. "He's old, he's not at all handsome, he behaves like a spoiled child; he's certainly oversexed. But see that worshipful look on Karen's face? That's what I looked like four years ago." She touched her face. "I can still feel it."

"You should leave him," Henry said.

"I will. I just have to work myself up to it."

Henry nodded and took a last drag of his cigarette. He ground it out on the sole of his sneaker and checked his watch. "Looks like no fireworks tonight."

"Not in this weather."

A distant bang and a high-pitched whine came from the direction of the bay.

"Oh!" Maisie said. "What do you know?"

Another bang, then the *rat-a-tat-tat* of several rockets going off in succession. They looked toward the bay and saw a faint geyser of stars shooting up through the fog.

ANYTHING CAN HAPPEN

ON THE MORNING IVAN HUMPHREY LOST HIS MIND, I was standing at
my kitchen window, which has a partial view of Ivan's backyard. I
wasn't looking at anything in particular, or thinking about anything
memorable. Probably I was drinking a cup of coffee and rinsing
some dishes in the sink. We had a red hummingbird feeder that
hung from the eave over the window, and in the summertime it
was alive with the tiny creatures, their wings whirring so fast as
to be almost invisible. But the feeder was empty that morning
because it was November, the Saturday before Thanksgiving. The
hummingbirds had fled to wherever hummingbirds flee, and it was
long past time for me to bring the feeder inside as it was made of
glass and would shatter in the cold.

That was yet another of the chores I hadn't gotten around to
since Terence moved out in September. The outdoor furniture
was still outdoors, blown hither and thither about the yard, and
the water in the above-ground pool we kept for the grandkids
had poisonous-looking algae and rotten brown leaves clotting the
surface of its water. It was a hazard, actually, and I knew I would
have to cover it before the holiday, when all five of the kids would
be here. They were still little enough then that they could have
fallen in and drowned—you heard stories like that all the time. The

cover should have been put on when the weather turned cool, but it was too heavy for me to lift. Terence always took care of that. I wasn't even sure where the cover was.

Seeing Ivan coming out his back door made me think I would ask him to do it, and maybe to mow the overgrown patch of lawn out front that had begun to look like I was cultivating wheat. We were friendly even though we weren't friends. He once borrowed a ladder from Terence. The houses in our neighborhood were built tight side by side; you knew nearly everyone at least to say hello, and many of our children had grown up together, so friendships were naturally formed. Often I joined the free tai chi class that met in the park across the street, which attracted people I knew from the neighborhood as well as strangers from other parts of town. If I had been looking out my front window instead of the window in back, I would have seen a group of middle-aged-to-old women and men moving in slow motion beneath a stand of lodgepole pines. I knew that my best friend Elaine was there; she was a fanatic who went every day. Tai chi is surprisingly difficult, as anyone who does it will tell you. We were lucky to have that park so close by. It had a nice playground in it, too.

I didn't know who Ivan's friends were, but I assumed he had a few. He was much younger than us, nearer to my children's age, and he and his wife didn't have kids. That in itself was odd in our neighborhood, where almost everyone had a family, but I wouldn't have said the Humphreys were unusual in any other way except Ivan was so thin that his ribs showed through his T-shirt, and his wife, Beryl, was obese. "Jack Sprat," Terence called Ivan. He called Beryl "Mama Cass."

I was about to stick my head out the back door and ask Ivan to help me with the pool, when I noticed he was holding a gun in the crook of his arm. Terence owned a gun. He enjoyed shooting birds in their season, but it was a long-barreled shotgun he'd inherited from his father that took cartridges instead of bullets. The shotgun was locked in a case in the basement so the grandkids couldn't get at it. Ivan was carrying the kind of gun you saw on TV, a handgun type but larger, about the length of a loaf of bread. It was shiny black, which is why I think I noticed it. Otherwise I would have mistaken it for a power tool of some kind and not thought anything about it.

I almost called out for Terence. He would have known what kind of gun it was. He enjoyed those shoot 'em up movies that were on TV at all hours, with Bruce Willis or whoever killing the bad guys while saving innocent citizens in impossible ways. This is not to say that I objected to Terence watching them, and it wouldn't have mattered if I had. Terence always did what he pleased, Melinda Poor being the most obvious example of that, and why I needed help with the pool.

I knew Terence was doing Melinda Poor ages before he told me, and when I say ages, I mean *years*, because that was how long it went on. Even our kids knew about Melinda. They'd met her and been to her condo; by the time they were teenagers they took it for granted that Melinda Poor was their father's girl. Melinda herself knew that I knew about her, so Terence was being disingenuous to say the very least when he "confessed" to me last Labor Day while I was watering the hydrangeas by the deck. He hoped I would kick him out, I think, so he wouldn't be blamed for leaving me. But I took the air right out of his tires. I didn't even stop watering.

"Oh, for goodness sake," I said. "I know all about you and Melinda. Everyone knows about it. You've been fooling around with her for fifteen years. Why on earth are you telling me now?"

He couldn't have expected me to be surprised, but I think he was prepared for me to be aggrieved. I had no intention of displaying my feelings; the time for that was long past. He said he planned to go live with Melinda in her condo at the opposite end of the park. Our youngest had married the spring before, and he thought that since all the kids were settled, he would go and live with her. He said he'd wanted to for quite a while but had our family to consider.

"You still have our family to consider," I said. We had four kids and five grandchildren who came over all the time. And I wasn't going to exist on nothing: he would have to continue to maintain my lifestyle and to pay the mortgage on the house. I couldn't imagine him living in Melinda's cramped condo with half his salary docked. He was a big man, tall and hefty, not old but getting there. I couldn't think what Melinda saw in him and had a sudden notion to phone her and ask.

I told him to go ahead and live with Melinda, if that's what he really wanted. I made him break it to the kids himself, and they were all disgusted. It's one thing to have a girlfriend on the side and another to leave your wife. He went off with just a couple of suitcases that didn't nearly hold all his stuff, so there were remnants of him all over the house that I hadn't found the energy to throw out.

Ivan Humphrey didn't do anything with the gun but hold it to his side. He appeared to be talking to himself, or if not to himself then to the ground. His grass was always perfect, like a putting green all year long. He sat down on the neatly stacked woodpile he kept by his back steps and shook his head like a dog in the rain. He banged his fist on his thigh. Finally he threw his head back and yelled, "Fuck it all!" I wouldn't have minded doing something similar myself, letting off steam. Then he got up from the woodpile and went inside his house. I went back to whatever I was doing, thinking I'd wait to ask him at a better time. I did notice he had shaved his head, but that was what balding men often did.

My daughter Cathy was coming over to help me make some pies for the homeless shelter's Thanksgiving. We did that every year. I was still in my bathrobe, and my hair was tangled from sleep. I looked at the clock. It was five to nine. Cathy was coming at nine-thirty, and she was always prompt. So I went upstairs and took a shower. Terence's Tegrin was still in the caddy that hung from the showerhead. He had dandruff, among other problems. His half-squeezed tube of Sensodyne remained on a shelf in the cabinet, and he must have bought a new stick of deodorant, because his Mennen was in there, too.

There are some people who think they have all the time in the world and then have to rush at the last minute and are late. I am the opposite, I never think I have enough time, and as a result I am always early. I am the one tapping my foot at the door, looking at my watch, and I've read more magazines in waiting rooms than anyone I know. When I had finished my shower and was dressed, it was only twenty past. So I relaxed for once and lingered at my vanity, putting on lipstick and styling my hair as I waited for Cathy to arrive. The vanity sat between my two bedroom windows. The Humphrey's windows were about ten feet away. But my curtains were white chiffon, which allowed for both privacy and light. So I didn't see anything, and I didn't look, but I could hear Ivan Humphrey's voice loud and clear even through the glass. He was screaming at his wife. He called her a "slut" and a "cunt" and a "goddamn idiot." He said she had ruined his life.

Beryl Humphrey's voice was barely audible and I couldn't make out what she said, but I know she talked back to Ivan because I heard him tell her to "shut the fuck up" and that he was "sick of her goddamn voice." I raised my eyebrows at myself in the mirror and thought that even though Terence was a cheater, he was never mean or abusive. If anything, he treated me better than most men treat their wives, except for the Melinda Poor thing. I always received a nice gift for my birthday and Christmas, and he never forgot our anniversary. He kissed me goodbye in the morning, and hello after work, and did everything I asked him to do around the house and the yard. I was contemplating this when I heard Cathy drive up. I pulled the curtain aside and saw her get out of her truck with a grocery bag full of canned pumpkin pie filling. At that exact minute I heard the loud *rat-tat-tat-tat* of what could have only been Ivan Humphrey's gun.

Since Cathy was so prompt, I could tell the police exactly when Ivan killed his wife. After that it probably took him thirty seconds to run downstairs, because Cathy was still standing on the sidewalk when Ivan burst out of his front door. So it was 9:31 when he shot my Cathy in the shoulder. She dropped the bag and fell to the pavement, cans of pumpkin pie filling rolling out into the street and her pink blouse turning red with blood. I don't know how fast I got down to her. She was conscious and able to talk. She told me to take her cell phone from her purse, which I did and called 911.

People started coming out of their houses to see what all the noise was about. Ivan Humphrey was walking down the street.

"Go back in!" I yelled. A number of people heard me and skedaddled back behind their doors. The rest of them stood like targets in a carnival game as Ivan Humphrey shot them with a few sweeps of his gun.

I was crying, though I was unaware of it until I saw my tears dripping onto the pavement. Sharon Beller from next door had tumbled down her front steps and lay upside down between a giant pumpkin and a sheaf of Indian corn she'd set out for the holiday. The top of her head had been shot off and there was nothing above her eyes.

"Don't look, Mom!" Cathy said. She was a sight herself. The flesh of her shoulder was blown to pieces and the joint showed white through the blood.

Once Ivan had reached the end of the block and shot everyone he could, he turned and started walking back toward where Cathy and I still were.

"Get under the car!" Cathy pushed me with her good hand and I did what she said. Oh, she was brave, my Cathy. She closed her eyes and pretended to be dead, and she looked it, with her skin chalky white and a greenish tint beneath her eyes.

Ivan's sneakers walked right up to Cathy's SUV, then turned away toward the park. I could see the tai chi group in the near distance, and the kids in the playground further on. Sometimes Cathy dropped her two boys at that playground when she came over to the house. I both did and didn't want to know whether she had done that this time. I asked her where they were.

"The playground," she whispered. "Jesus God."

"I'll get them." I started wriggling out from under the car.

"No, Mom!" she said. "He'll kill you!"

I really didn't care whether Ivan Humphrey killed me or not as long as he left my grandkids alone. I had lived a full life and didn't expect it to get any better. I crawled out from under the car and ran to the north side of the park. There was a forest of rhododendron there that I thought I would use as cover. Ivan had a head start on me, so I ran along through the bushes as fast as I could, the sappy leaves slapping my face and leaving their stickiness on my skin.

The tai chi group saw him coming. Some of them, the way some of my neighbors had, stood still with fear and shock, while others ran in the opposite direction from the playground, taking cover from pine to pine. They knew, as I did, where Ivan would go next if he were crazy and evil enough. Elaine was one of those who tried to redirect Ivan's path. He turned and walked toward the tree she was hiding behind. She ran out and he shot her dead. It was all I could do not to rush over to her. Elaine, my best and oldest friend. She lay on the pine needles like a fallen princess, her face resting on one arm, blood seeping through the white terry yoga outfit I gave her for her birthday last July.

I clapped my hand over my mouth and heaved uncontrollable sobs. I stepped further back into the bushes in case Ivan heard me cry. He shot the Lings, an elderly Chinese couple who couldn't have run if they'd tried. I saw that Claire Winkle from my church was dead, as was Julian Goldman, who had recently retired. There was blood on the ground where Ivan's victims lay, and blood splattered on his jeans and shirt. It wasn't an ordinary gun he was using: it tore people apart. As he turned away from my direction and searched for anyone he'd missed, the sunlight filtering through the pines made his bare head appear to glow.

I took the opportunity to come out of the bushes and race across the grass to the kids.

I heard sirens; Ivan must have heard them, too. The sound gave me a feeling of relief. Help would be here soon. As soon as I thought that, I felt a terrible pain in my thigh. I stumbled, looked down, and saw blood. Leg wounds can kill you, particularly if they're in the thigh, because that's where an important artery lies and you can bleed to death if it's severed. Terence had told me that when he was a volunteer fireman. He was required to know that sort of information, as well as how to put out fires. That's how he met Melinda Poor, in fact. She was an EMT.

So I'm going to die now, I thought, as the blood streamed down my pants and puddled in my shoe. The wound went straight through from back to front. Cathy's sons were on the slide in the playground, the older one holding his little brother on his lap so he wouldn't fall into the dirt at the bottom. I looked behind me and saw that Ivan had shot me from some distance. I found out later that if he'd been any closer I might have lost my leg.

I couldn't run, but I could still walk. I'd take a step with my good leg and drag the hurt one along. I was bleeding hard, and I was scared, but I didn't want to frighten the kids any more than was necessary to make them hear me and obey.

"Run, kids! Run that way!" I pointed. "Go to the fountain at the end of the park. Quickly, quickly!" I clapped my hands. I thanked the Lord when they started jumping off the swings and the slide and the seesaw, the merry-go-round and the jungle gym. They did exactly what I told them to do, which was a miracle if you know kids. They ran in a scrambling, screaming, colorful pack away from Ivan Humphrey's gun.

As my job was done, I lay down on the grass. I wept in sorrow, but I was also so glad. I closed my eyes and waited for Ivan to come. The November sun was surprisingly warm, though the ground beneath me was cold. Then the sun disappeared and my skin felt chilly. I could tell someone was there.

"Melinda. I expected Ivan Humphrey."

"He's dead," she said. "Suicide by cop."

"I'm alive."

"You are." She smiled at me, and I could see why Terence liked her so much. She wasn't pretty, but she had a way about her, something humorous and matter-of-fact. She expertly tied a rubber tourniquet tight around my upper thigh.

"You're lucky," she said.

"I know it."

"Cathy is on her way to the hospital. I called Terence to pick up her boys. They went where you told them to go, all the kids. They're at the fountain at the end of the park."

I could see the ambulance coming for me, driving over the grass. The walkie-talkie on Melinda's belt mumbled and barked incoherently.

"You like living with Terence?" I said.

"Hah. Do me a favor." She snapped off her latex gloves. "Take him back and keep him, okay? He's driving me up a wall."

I made Terence take me to every funeral, even Ivan Humphrey's. I checked out of the hospital after my surgery and had him push me around town in a wheelchair. I would have to have a second surgery, but that was a few weeks away. Cathy had three surgeries total, and she was able to keep her arm, but she couldn't raise it above her waist, and her shoulder was sunken and scarred. Twelve people were killed, so that made thirteen funerals including Ivan's. Nobody went to Ivan's service but me and Terence and Ivan's mother.

"Who are you?" she said as Terence bumped me up the church steps with my hurt leg sticking out in front of me. She wasn't nearly as old as she should have been. She must have given birth to Ivan when she was a girl. She stood beside the church door, smoking a cigarette. It was raining and her hair was wet. She wore a faux leopard coat that was wet as well, its nap separated in little clumps.

"We were his neighbors," I said. "He shot my daughter and killed my best friend."

"Among others," Terence said. He moved impatiently from foot to foot. He didn't think Ivan deserved a funeral. But Ivan had been a regular person once. He didn't lose his mind on purpose.

"Why are you here?" she said. She wasn't defensive. It was just a question.

"I don't know. I felt I had to. I saw him kill almost everyone who died."

"I can't tell you why he did it. It is as much a mystery to me as it is to you. I won't pretend he had a perfect childhood, but who does? He went and lived with his late father after he turned sixteen. I didn't know much about him after that." She pointed at my bandaged leg. "He did that to you?"

"Yes."

"I'm sorry. You're the only victim I've been able to say that to. I'm sorry about your friend and your daughter, too."

"My daughter's alive, thank the Lord."

"Anything can happen," she said. "You forget that, until it does."

After the service, Terence and I went home. He moved back in while I was in the hospital, but I made no mention of the fact. I behaved as if he'd never left. Maybe it stung when Melinda kicked him out, or maybe he was glad to be home. I wasn't going to probe. His pride and my pride were equal now, weights on a balanced scale. The cover was on the pool, and the outdoor furniture was stacked in the garage. The glass hummingbird feeder still swung from the eave because it had always been my job to take it down, but I wasn't going to be able to do that for a while, so I took the chance that it might break in the cold.

MYRNA ATHENA

"DID YOU SEE THAT?" Myrna says in that voice of hers, a raspy screech just short of loud. She's standing by the floor-to-ceiling window at the south end of the office, the one with a partial view of the river. We're on the tenth floor, and my cubicle is four rows in, so I can't see much. I keep working as if I haven't heard her, but her face is in my line of sight and she's plenty agitated. I've always thought she looks like her voice: frizzy red hair, dowel legs, sharp little elbows, pre-teen breasts. She wears sweaters on top of sweaters—"sweater sets," my wife says they're called—even though it's sweltering. They crank up the heat from September through May, then the air-conditioning kicks in and we freeze all summer long.

George Wild is the first to pop up from his cubicle, a chinless jack-in-the-box. "What?" he says. "See what?" Then heads are popping up all over the room. People are walking over to the window.

"A man just now jumped off the top of the building across the street. I saw him do it! I was standing here enjoying the view and finishing my yogurt from lunch." Myrna holds up the empty carton, exhibit A, as if what she was eating has anything to do with it. "He came out of that door beneath the water tower and went off the edge of the roof right there." She presses her forehead against the window, her nose-breath fogging the glass. "There he is on the sidewalk! Oh my God, how awful."

"So much blood!" Elaine Yen says. "It looks like he's floating in it."

This is too much for me. I have to get up and look. I squeeze through the group and stand in front of the window.

"There," Myrna says. She doesn't need to point. It's obvious. A crowd has already gathered. The guy is lying on his back, enclosed in an amoeba of blood. Otherwise he looks strangely unharmed. I imagine him standing up and walking away.

"He jumped?" I say stupidly.

"Well, not really, that was the odd thing, he didn't actually jump. He sort of strolled off, as if he didn't realize the roof ended there."

"How sick," says Gervaise Hoff. "You watched a man kill himself." She's Steve's secretary, or assistant, or whatever they call it. I don't have one myself. She loathes us all, that's obvious—and her job too, because she's always threatening to quit. She's wearing acid green tights and a tiny orange skirt, her golden hair shining like a kid's in the sun.

"Well, what was I supposed to do, Gervaise?" Myrna says. "Cover my eyes? It happened in a flash."

An ambulance and a few police cars arrive. The crowd is encouraged to stand back. The paramedics zip the guy into a bag and heft him onto a gurney. The ambulance drives away without a siren, its red light rotating sluggishly.

"Show's over, folks," Steve says. I could do his job with my hands tied behind my back, but that isn't the way things work. Cheerful idiots run whole divisions and hang on until retirement, while the competent people are the first ones to be laid off, or fired if they're unpopular. He tells Myrna to take the rest of the day, so she puts on her fuzzy plaid overcoat and leaves, and the rest of us go back to our cubes.

I tell Frances about it as soon as I get home. She's a nurse and works nights, so she's just woken up and is flipping pancakes for her breakfast. She doesn't know the people in my office, but she's heard enough about everyone to follow the stories I bring home.

"Myrna said it seemed like he didn't do it on purpose," I say. "He was walking across the roof and he just kept walking—'strolling,' she said—as if he didn't see the edge."

"That's absurd. Of course he knew what he was doing." She frowns at a pancake she's scooping off the griddle. "Unless he was blind. Was he blind?"

"He got up to the roof by himself."

"He probably had decided to do it and didn't want to pause and think about it anymore."

"That makes sense," I say. Frances always has an answer to whatever question is posed. When I married her she was whippet-thin and so articulate as to be intimidating. She has plumped up considerably since then, but she's still smarter than anyone I know.

"If I were to kill myself, I wouldn't jump off a building," she says. "Too much time for regret going down."

"You would never kill yourself."

"True. But a lot of mentally ill patients come into the hospital, so I know how badly a person can suffer in their mind." She takes a bite of pancake and talks through the food. "People take their lives every day."

"If you had seen this guy lying on the street, you wouldn't have believed it. I didn't know there was that much blood in a body."

"Ten pints. But an accident victim, like your man on the roof, can require as much as ten times that to be revived. That is, if he's not already dead, which I assume your guy was. More than five stories is a fatal fall." That's the kind of information she knows from being a nurse in an emergency room.

After Frances leaves for the hospital, I heat up a Lean Cuisine and turn on the TV in the extra bedroom we use as a computer room and den. There's no reason for me to feel mournful, I didn't even know the roof guy, but I'm not interested in my usual TV shows and I can't settle down. I keep imagining it was me who stepped off the edge of that roof. Looking down at the guy from the tenth floor, it was impossible to make out his facial features, but I could see he was dark-haired, like me, and he was wearing, as I was, a suit and tie. Like a million other men, I remind myself; like practically every guy in my office. Still, it gives me a shock to realize that someone who, at least superficially, wasn't so different from me, would choose oblivion over the pleasures of life, however small those pleasures might be.

I go to the computer and google *man jumps from roof downtown*. A lot of useless garbage comes up, so I go to the website of the local newspaper and type the same words into their search box. I figure it's too early for anything to have been written because I don't get any matches. In the morning the story will be on the front page, and everything about the guy will be revealed: his name and occupation, his wife's name, his kids and siblings and parents. "Survived by," as they say in the obituaries, meaning the guy's next of kin, though it occurs to me that if you're dead you're "survived by" every living thing on earth from elephants on down to algae.

Since I'm at the computer anyway, I google Myrna. I don't expect to find anything, but her phone number and address come up under her bizarre full name: Myrna Athena Bierce. I attach my Bluetooth to my ear and tap her number into my cell. Either she's just hung up from talking to someone, or is expecting the phone to ring, because she answers immediately in a pert phone-answering voice even though it's after ten.

"I'm fine," she says before I ask. "Yes, I was very shaken up this afternoon, but everyone has been so nice, calling me to see how I'm doing. It's always helpful to be able to talk things out when you're feeling upset."

I mute the TV, then turn it off altogether. "People from the office have been calling you?"

"Oh gosh, yes. Steve and Elaine, and George, of course. He's such a good man, George. Harrison in Marketing, and Melissa from Reception. Why, I even heard from Gervaise!"

"Gervaise! What did she want?"

"She was sweet. She apologized for speaking thoughtlessly. She said that death 'freaked her out,' and I can well imagine why, what with her brother killing her father on the family farm that way."

"*What* way?" I say. I don't know jack about Gervaise, but the last thing I would have suspected about her is that she grew up on a farm.

"Her brother ran over their father with a combine harvester. He was backing up and didn't see their father standing behind the machine, and their father was looking the other way and didn't see it coming. Gervaise's brother wasn't checking the rear view because he assumed he had a clear path. Gervaise saw it happen. Terrible. We had a long talk about it."

I didn't realize that Myrna is so popular with our colleagues. I assumed she was universally annoying. I can't tell if she is surprised to hear from me. It's me who's surprised to hear who else has called, and even more surprised at myself for calling.

"So you're feeling OK now," I say.

"Well, I wouldn't say *okay*! I'll be thinking about what I saw for a long time. I can't understand what would make a person do that. And then seeing him on the street. He didn't really look dead, I thought."

"That's what I thought too! I even imagined he might still be alive. I wonder if that's denial. My wife thinks I'm in denial a lot. Like when the plane went into the World Trade Center? I thought, oh, they can fix that. Here's all this black smoke billowing out of the building and I'm like, it's not *that* bad. She says because I watch so much violent TV, real traumas don't affect me very deeply."

"Oh, no," Myrna says. "I know that's not true because you wouldn't have called me if you weren't upset by what happened this afternoon."

"I'm not upset. I called you to see how you're holding up."

"Honestly?" Myrna's voice is truly screechy.

I get up and walk into the long narrow hall off the den that leads from the kitchen to our bedroom. Frances is always talking about hanging photographs on the walls, but we've owned the house for two and a half years and haven't done it so far.

"Okay, I admit I'm preoccupied by it," I say. "The guy...well, he kind of looked like me, and I keep imagining he *is* me, or rather I'm him, jumping off the roof. I can't help wondering about his life, you know? Like was he married, did he have kids?" I look at my fingernails, which need clipping. There's a pen mark on the ball of my thumb. Sometimes I doodle on the palm of my hand, though mostly I doodle on paper. A little known fact about me is that I majored in art at college.

"Do you have kids?" Myrna says.

"No," I say, and add, "Not yet." Why I say "not yet" I don't know, because we don't plan to have kids ever. One of the things Frances and I have in common is we both had horrible parents. Mine were raging, angry alcoholics; hers were neglectful and abusive in turns. Neither of us can stand the idea of reliving a particle of our childhoods through being parents ourselves. "Another thing I wonder is what he did, what his job was. Did he like it? Was he successful? Or did he wish he did something else?"

"Like you," Myrna says.

"Like me what?" I'm in the kitchen, looking in the fridge for something to snack on. It's what I always do, eat hardly anything for dinner, then get hungry later and gorge myself. Frances knows this, plus she likes to eat, too, so the fridge is always bursting with food. There's a chicken on the second shelf that I pull a leg off of. I spoon a mound of chocolate ice cream into a bowl. I'm getting fatter and so is Frances, but we aren't fat enough yet to gross each other out.

"You wish you did something else," Myrna says. "Don't worry, it's not obvious, but I have always sensed that your heart's not in your work. If you could do anything you choose, what would you do?"

That's a no-brainer. "I would move to Italy and paint for the rest of my life."

Myrna's delighted. "Oh, imagine!" she says. "Grapevines on a hill, dark cypress trees. A stone house."

"With an arbor and a pond. And I would eat pasta every day."

"Perfect. And your wife? What would she do? Grow roses and have babies?"

This stops me. Frances has never figured in my Italy fantasy. She would hate living outside the US, for one thing, and she goes to her job at the hospital every evening with a bustling determination that shows she can't wait to get there.

"My wife is very practical," I say. "And truthfully, we don't plan on having kids."

"I didn't think so," Myrna says.

"Why do you say that?"

"You told me once that you've been married for six years. If you were going to have children you would have done it already."

"We still can."

"Absolutely you can."

I take my ice cream and sit in the dark living room. Sometimes I wish we had children, especially during the holidays. Frances and I go to the movies on Thanksgiving and usually take a cruise between Christmas and New Year's. If I liked my job, I might not think about it—I know Frances doesn't—but it's lonely sometimes, not having any family.

"It isn't a very original fantasy," I say. "But that's what I would do if I could. What about you?"

"I would live in a hut on the beach in Goa and swim in the Indian Ocean every day."

"Goa?"

"It's a town in India on the sea. I've always wanted to go there. They have wonderful diving, I hear."

"You scuba dive?"

"I got my license a few years ago. It's great fun, you should try it."

I put my feet up on the coffee table and imagine Myrna scuba diving, moving slowly down and down through green water glittering with colorful fish, her skinny legs scissoring and her frizzy hair floating, her freckled face obscured by a mask.

"I never learned to swim," I say. "My parents didn't teach me and I didn't go to camp or anything. They were assholes, my parents. I don't know how to ride a bike, either. They taught me how to make a martini, though." Suddenly I want to make a martini. I go back into the kitchen and get out some gin and vermouth and find a Tupperware pitcher to use as a shaker.

"Let me tell you how," I say as I pour the gin into the Tupperware and follow it with a splash of vermouth. I dump in a load of ice.

"How to make a martini?" Myrna says. "I know how to do that. I learned from a bartender at the Waldorf when I lived in New York."

"Bullshit!" I say. "You lived in New York? I always wanted to live in New York." I put the top on the pitcher and shake it.

"Only for a few years. I had a ball, but I was ready to come home."

There's plenty left over even after I pour myself a generous drink. I take the glass and the pitcher back to the living room.

"Okay," I say. "You have to tell me. How did you get your middle name?"

"I found it in a book of Greek myths when I was a child. Athena is the goddess of wisdom. I liked it, so I gave it to myself. My middle name was Lynnette, which I hated."

"Myrna Lynnette," I say. I make a face.

"Exactly," she says, as if she can see me.

The martini is smooth and I'm enjoying it, but I'm such a lightweight that it's going straight to my head.

"I think you made the right choice," I say. "About the name."

"Yes, I think so too. It's certainly a conversation piece."

"I forgot how much I like martinis. I made a whole pitcher of them."

"Well, don't drink it all, for goodness sake! You'll feel terrible tomorrow morning."

The thought of tomorrow morning makes me want to break something. Lately, preparing for the day has become a chore so dispiriting that I have to force myself to open my eyes. I can hardly find the energy to squeeze the toothpaste onto the brush. The shower takes ages to warm up while I hop around naked on the cold tiles, and instead of using a washcloth, Frances makes me "exfoliate" with a loofah. She wants me to put on moisturizer, too, which I never do. The time it takes to wash and then dress my widening body is about as long as I care to think about it. Because I don't read the paper, I listen to the news on the way to work. Frances loves the news. Nothing happens that she isn't up on, which is the reason I turn on the radio, to have some idea of what she's talking about. I probably should have married an ignorant woman who doesn't care about soft skin, because the morning news and exfoliation are two things I can live without. Another thing I'd like to eliminate is riding the elevator at work, because if there is anyone in there who I have to talk to, my mood goes from gloomy to crap.

Now I am getting tipsy; two martinis are my limit. My parents would drink five or six of them before they crossed the threshold to crazy. Then they'd go at each other like fighting cocks, and at me, too, if I didn't escape. Later, they would pass out in places that made me wonder what they'd been doing: halfway up the stairs, or on the kitchen floor, and once in the front yard, side by side on their backs. That time I had to revive them in case they froze to death overnight, but usually I just left them where they lay, only to wake up the next day to my mother frying eggs and my father eating them as if they'd never said a cross word to each other.

"I always feel terrible in the morning," I say. "Maybe if I drank martinis every night I'd feel better."

"Oh, I doubt that. I don't take you for a drinking man."

"What kind of man do you take me for?" Never in my life have I wondered what Myrna Bierce thinks of me, but now I really want to know.

"Truthfully, I don't know you well enough to say what kind of man you are. I only want to keep you from drinking too much and coming into the office with a hangover. Alcohol is a depressant, and you're sad enough, don't you think?"

"Sad!" I'm astonished. "*You* think *I'm* sad? You're the one that's sad." I sit up and put my drink on the table beside me. "A sad old maid is what you are. Goa! Right. Like you'll ever get to India. What a crock. I really feel sorry for you."

"Oh, now," Myrna says. "I'll forget this conversation ever happened, and I'll see you at the office tomorrow." Politely, she says goodnight and then the line goes dead.

It takes me a moment to understand that she isn't there anymore. Every now and then I fly off the handle and act like a prick for no good reason. Frances thinks I can't help myself because my parents were that way. "The apple doesn't fall far from the tree," is her stock cliché. I could say the same about her because she isn't the most loving person in the world. She has a whiplash tongue that I go out of my way to avoid.

I redial Myrna's number and listen to it ring, then pour the rest of the martinis into the kitchen sink and go back to the dark living room. I wait there, doing nothing, listening to my wristwatch tick. Around three o'clock I call Myrna again, and she answers in a sleepy voice.

"You're right," I say. "I am sad."

"Of course you are."

I ask her to talk to me until the sun rises, so I won't have to wake up in the morning. She says she will, and she does: we talk about everything that enters our minds. Frances comes home around five o'clock and is alarmed to see me up.

"Is that your wife? Well, then I'll let you go," Myrna says, as if she's the one keeping me. But I don't want her to let me go. I want to hang on forever.

Mrs. Temple

On the boat ride from the mainland to St. Jude, Helena was the only person who sat out on deck enjoying the glittering, teal-blue sea and the sun beating hot on her face. The rest of the passengers huddled beneath the canvas overhang, protecting themselves from the very elements they had come to the Islands to enjoy. She looked at them and they looked at her. There were two older couples and one young couple and an infant in a stroller. A uniformed crewman came out to her. His face was so black against his brilliant white shirt that she could hardly make out his features.

"You'll get wet out here," he said, indicating the chop and the boat's foaming wake. The boat always went very fast, rearing up at the bow like a whale.

"I don't mind." She shook the wind through her blonde hair. She had already been sprayed, a pleasant spritz. "It's nice, it feels good." She wasn't one of those hapless tourists with their SPF shirts and sun visors, their backpacks and bursting totes. She wore a cream blouse and linen trousers; her large leather handbag, also cream, was a serene companion beside her. "I always sit here, I'm an old hand. I've been coming to St. Jude for years! But I don't recognize you—or do I? No, you must be new." She smiled. "What's happened to Lionel? And George?"

"Lionel took a job on the mainland," he said. "George passed away."

"Oh!" Helena said. Though George had been the captain of the boat for as long as she could remember, she'd never really spoken to him except to say hello and goodbye. The crewman didn't tell her what he died of and she didn't want to ask. She would bring it up later with Desiree, the manager of the resort, who would be waiting on the dock as usual to greet the guests as they disembarked. Desiree would wonder why Helena was alone. *What's happened to Mr. Temple?* she would ask in her musical voice. She was a round and glossy woman with a headful of dancing braids. Helena planned to say that Mr. Temple was delayed on business. It seemed like the simplest excuse. Mr. Temple, Larry, her husband of three years, had announced a few days earlier that he was seeing a younger woman.

"Oh, Larry, how banal," she'd said. She would have been embarrassed for him if she hadn't been so dismayed. He approached all things new with puerile enthusiasm and scant attention, his desires and interests clattering around like trapped birds from wall to wall to wall. He was rich and not very smart because he'd never tried to be. "Do you really want to be married seven times? Aren't you exhausted by now?" She had believed, when they married, that she would be his last wife. She thought they were fond of each other. He was her second husband after a brief marriage in her twenties and thirty years of unattainable men.

"I want an heir," he said, as if revealing a lofty goal.

"You'll be dead by the time it goes to college," she said. "How do you know she can give you one, anyway?"

He knew because the woman was pregnant. He was so pleased that he had been able to knock someone up that he giggled when he told her.

"I'm Mrs. Temple," she said to the crewman. "It's very nice to meet you." She put out her hand. He took it but didn't shake it. She realized he thought she was asking him to help her get up and go beneath the overhang. "No, no, I really am fine. Besides, we're almost there."

A wooden dock, silvery with age, extended from a fragment of beach. A white woman waited at the end. Helena squinted. Where was Desiree?

"Retired," the crewman said.

"But she's too young to retire!" Helena said.

The crewman laughed. "She's sixty!"

"Well, she looks a good deal younger that."

"No, Dessie's an old lady," he said.

Helena was fifty-nine. "Just wait until you're sixty. Believe me, you won't think of yourself as old."

The boat drew parallel to the dock and the crewman threw out a line; Desiree's replacement handily caught it and wrapped it around a pylon. Deeply tanned, her long hair bleached white by the sun, she wore a tank top and very brief khaki shorts and flip-flops. As the passengers disembarked, she herded them up the dock. No one would be asking where Mr. Temple was, or greeting Helena like an old friend.

It never rained on St. Jude in February, not in Helena's memory. Sipping coffee on the tiny beachfront terrace outside her room, she watched the sky brighten from watercolor pink to an impenetrable blue, while the silhouettes of the palm trees grew sharp on the sand. The sea flowed from cerulean to robin's egg to celadon green, like samples of paint on a wall. She wondered if Larry would let her have their apartment, which she had redecorated only last year. Nothing too feminine, but not masculine either, she'd relied heavily on blues and greens. The apartment was originally Larry's, a two-bedroom on the park, but the girlfriend would doubtless want something larger, with a garden for the child. Helena sighed. Larry would be a terrible father. He hated noise and mess and, most of all, obligations. She doubted the girlfriend knew that. "A new broom sweeps clean," she said to herself. By the time she really got to know Larry he was trailing swathes of dust, but she hadn't minded, she'd been glad to be married.

She heard the scraping of a chair on the terrace of the room next door, which was hidden by a stucco partition.

"Here you go," a man's voice said. "Is that coffee too hot?" A mumbled response. The clink of cutlery on china. The man's voice again: "Beautiful morning, isn't it?"

"Hello!" Helena called out. "I'm your next-door neighbor."

"Excuse me, ma'am?" the man said.

"I'm your next door neighbor! I'm sorry to interrupt you. I just thought I'd let you know I'm here."

"The guest next door," he said to the mumbler. "Well, thank you, ma'am. I hope we didn't bother you."

"Oh, no, not at all!" Helena said. She waited for him to say something else. When he didn't, she finished her coffee and went inside to change into a bathing suit.

She'd made an effort, all these years, to keep her figure slim as she watched her married friends thicken—because looks were beside the point, weren't they, once you'd scored a husband and produced a family. When she was unmarried those women had pitied her; now they would pity her again. She examined her body in the bathroom mirror. No amount of crunches could keep the flesh of her abdomen from looking like a curtain poised to drop. Her breasts hung slack, dimples pocked her ass, her elbows were whirlpools of sag. She examined the wrinkles around her mouth that lipstick seeped into by the end of every day like blood into capillaries. Overnight, it seemed, she had developed a wattle beneath her chin. She felt as if she was enclosed in an extraneous layer of skin. "What you need is a plastic surgeon," she said as she pulled her face taut with both hands. She imagined being sliced from head to toe and emerging fresh from herself.

Her ritual was to walk to the north end of the beach in the morning and the south end after lunch. She kicked off her espadrilles at the edge of the sand and walked just shy of the breaking waves. The beach was long, half a mile each way, skirted by jungle and ending at a huge berm of rocks that sucked the sea into dramatic geysers. Helena's feet sunk into the flat pink sand, leaving the only prints on the beach. She liked to walk when no one else was yet out. There was a singular anxiety to meeting another walker on the beach—watching them steadily approach and knowing you would be obliged to greet them. She wondered why this was so. They were only people, not oncoming trains. Social anxiety her former therapist called it, *anticipatory* anxiety. And yet she was known for being gregarious, charming and popular, invited to everything and always talking on the phone. "You're a people-pleaser," her therapist once said in the days when she was still single. "Well, I have to be, don't I," she'd countered.

She felt her stamina flag, and slowed her pace to a stroll. She'd been up half the night listening to the crash of the waves and trying to work out her future. There wouldn't be any problem about money; Larry wasn't cheap. She wouldn't have to find a job, go back to work, which would be impossible at her age anyway. If she could keep the apartment, just remain where she was, she thought she would be all right. She supposed her dating days were all but over, though perhaps she would be surprised. A palm reader she'd consulted after the demise of her first marriage told her she would be married twice, and at the time she'd been happy to hear it. Now it was like a death sentence. She would be alone for the rest of her life.

Reaching the end of the beach, she stopped short of where the waves roared into the rocks and spewed up fearsome fountains. She covered her face with her hands and dropped to her knees and wept inaudibly for herself, heaving and trembling and bowing so low that her hair left shallow tracks in the sand. All her life, she'd been such a good sport! But she had lost the spirit, the cheerful face, the being attractive and out and about. She raised her head and wailed at the sky until she ran out of breath. The waves kicked up a fine, cool mist that kissed her face and arms. The problem was that life went on no matter how you felt about it.

After several minutes, she stood up and briskly brushed the sand from her legs. A man approached from the opposite direction near enough to have seen her. So what, she thought, lots of people sat on the beach. She could have been looking at a shell. She put on her sunglasses and strode purposefully toward him, prepared to say hello.

"Is that your grandfather you're with?" she asked the man next door as they teetered on rickety stools at the bar. His name was Daniel Booker and he was from Montgomery, Alabama. "Never mind. It's none of my business." People had all sorts of unconventional relationships these days; for all she knew they were lovers. She'd seen them at dinner the night before, and walking arm in arm that afternoon, the old man hunched and vague-eyed, his legs beneath the hems of his Bermuda shorts strangely bloated as if his essence had given in to gravity. She'd already gathered from listening to Daniel's voice next door that he was from the South, his accent thick enough to bend every word he said. His face looked weather-beaten. He wasn't young but he wasn't old. She liked the way his hair flopped over his forehead, glossy, dark and straight.

"No, he's my father," Daniel said.

Helena raised her eyebrows. "Really. How old is he? If you don't mind my asking."

"Ninety-two. He was fifty-seven when I was born. My mother died two years ago. We didn't expect her to go first. So now I take care of him. We used to come here when I was growing up, and I thought it would be nice to come back. The place hasn't changed at all."

"Not a bit," Helena said. She took a sip of her drink, a mojito, deliciously sweet and minty. "I've been coming here for years. Through thick and thin, always a week in St. Jude. When I was young, much younger than you, I used to scrape and save all year long to be able to afford the trip."

"But no more," he said.

"No, I'm all grown up now." She looked at her hands, at the rings Larry had given her: a chunky gold dome and a sapphire band, and the large square-cut diamond that was her engagement ring. She'd come to the bar because she was lonely in her room, exhausted but alert as an owl. Daniel was there already. They sat at the bar and talked the way strangers do, telling bits and pieces about themselves, holding back and letting go.

"My soon-to-be former husband is expecting a baby. He's sixty-one." She looked at Daniel. He clearly didn't know what to say. "An older father, like yours. Hopefully he'll live to see his child into adulthood. I don't know why I say *hopefully* when I don't actually care. It's his first. And his only, I assume, but stranger things have happened, I might be proven wrong."

"My father was in the military," Daniel said. "He says that's why he married so late, he was too busy fighting wars. World War Two. Then, later, Korea."

"You're proud of him," she said.

"He's the finest man I've ever known."

She had to turn away from the emotion in his voice. "I don't think," she said to the wall, "that my husband's child will feel the same way."

"You don't like him much, I guess."

"No, that's not true. I'm very fond of him, for all his sins." She realized that Larry's baby would grow up and take care of him. "I'm sorry," she said. "I'm in sort of a bad state. I didn't expect anyone to be here this late." She was getting drunk. No, she was beyond getting. She'd already downed two tiny bottles of scotch from the minibar in her room.

"Would you like me to leave?" He rose from his seat.

"No, I didn't mean that. I meant that I was unprepared for socializing. Normally I'm a lot of fun." She asked the bartender for another drink.

"Would you like to come down to the beach with me?" Daniel said. "I was about to go there when you came in. The moon is full. I wanted to see it reflected on the water."

Helena drew back, half-joking. "Are you propositioning me?"

"Of course not."

She sucked the dregs of her mojito. One more and she thought she would vomit. "Of *course* not. What does that mean? You're not attracted to me?"

"With all due respect ma'am, no I am not." He stood beautifully erect. She had offended him.

"Well, I am not unattractive. And don't call me *ma'am*. It makes me feel a thousand years old."

He considered her. "May I help you to your room?"

"How old do you think I am?"

"I'm not thinking about your age."

"Oh, I can get a lot drunker than this."

"Goodnight, then," he said.

She watched him walk away. "Are you married?" she called out. If he heard her, he didn't answer.

A few minutes later, she got up to go and immediately tripped and fell on the terracotta floor. The bartender was helping her up before she knew what had happened.

"Oh, Jesus," he said, and held a cocktail napkin to her chin. "You're bleeding." He set her on her feet like a doll. "You okay? What's your name, missus? You know how to get to your room?"

"My name is Mrs. Temple," she annunciated. "I know exactly where I am."

She did end up vomiting, and passing out on the bed. In the morning she was alarmed to find a streak of blood on the sheets until she remembered the night before. She found some Band-Aids and patched herself up, and spent the day on a beach chaise beneath a large hat. Around noon, Desiree's replacement appeared at her feet.

"Mrs. Temple. Hi, I'm Becky, the resort manager. We met when you arrived?" She wore a red bikini top and a pair of cut-off denim shorts. Her white-blond hair snaked over one shoulder in a loose braid that was punctuated by a red hibiscus flower. "I understand you had an accident up at the bar last night."

"It's sweet of you to be concerned," Helena said. "But not to worry, I'm fine."

"I'm so glad. Due to the fact that you were intoxicated, the resort cannot be found liable. But we would like you to come to the office and sign papers to that effect. Just a formality, you know."

"No, I don't know. What makes you think I was intoxicated?"

Becky put her hands on her hips and looked down the beach. "Joshua says he served you four mojitos."

Helena took off her sunglasses. "And that leads you to believe I was intoxicated." She had no idea why she was arguing this. There was something infuriating about the way Becky said *intoxicated* as if it had a question mark at its end. "You're relying on Joshua's opinion, I take it? His word against mine?"

"I don't want to embarrass you, Mrs. Temple, but Joshua says that a gentleman, Mr. Booker, was also present minutes before you fell. I would prefer not to have to ask Mr. Booker what state you were in, but if I must—"

"Please do! I'm not in the least embarrassed. Let me know what he says."

"Seriously, Mrs. Temple?" Becky's sun-browned forehead collapsed into creases.

"Seriously." She watched from behind her sunglasses as Becky marched up and knocked on the door of Daniel's room. Daniel came out. Becky talked. Daniel shook his head. He was either saying it was a shame that Helena drank so much, or telling Becky that Joshua was mistaken. Helena blinked as Becky walked away. Daniel looked out at her and waved a cheerful hello, went back in and closed the door.

Becky did not return. Helena fell into a sweaty doze, kept half-conscious by the sound of the waves and the clack of the palm leaves above her. People she'd never seen before populated her dreams, speaking to each other in voices she couldn't hear. A small dog carried a much larger dog on its back. Helena understood that something was the matter with the large dog and that she was meant to lead it to safety, but where safety could be found and what was wrong with the dog were troubling mysteries, and then the dogs were gone.

She woke to find Daniel sitting on the sand beside her, looking out at the sea.

"Thank you," she said. "For lying for me. You didn't have to. I don't know why I denied I was drunk. I *was* drunk. And I'm sorry I

65

was so rude to you last night. As I said, I'm having a bit of a rough time." She took off her sunglasses and made a rueful face. "Middle-aged lush falls on her chin."

"No need to apologize," he said. "I know about having a rough time. People avoid you, but what you really need is company and kindness."

"Yes, I suppose that's true. I do feel a bit like a pariah. Shunned, I suppose would be the word. I don't expect anyone to be kind to me. People just aren't. Not to women my age. Women become invisible once they're not young anymore." She smiled at him. "But I digress. You're nice, is what I mean to say."

"Understanding," he said. "Polite. I'm not really all that nice." He continued to look out at the water as he spoke. His face was sharper in profile than it appeared to be straight on, the lines of his nose and jaw were sharp. "I was married, and my wife left me, so I get it. It's humiliating. It takes a long time to get over."

"It's horrible," Helena said. "Do you mind if I ask what happened?"

"I was away a lot, for long periods of time. She met someone else and fell in love with him." He looked at her, finally. "Hey, I'm going swimming, you want to join me?" He took off his shirt. His upper body was crisscrossed with scars, pink as worms or flat and pale, melded like hot metal over much of his chest, jagged on his arms and back.

Helena had never seen anything like it. "What on earth happened to you?" she asked before she could stop herself. She put a hand to her mouth. "Oh, I'm sorry."

"No, that's okay. They're shrapnel wounds. Iraq. I was in the army, like my father. And my grandfather, and my great-grandfather." He twisted around, looking at the scars. "They're ugly, but I'm alive, which is more than I can say for many."

"Iraq," Helena said.

He watched her. "Go ahead, you can touch them."

She reached out and traced a triangular gash on his arm. "How?" she said.

"It was just a routine reconnaissance mission. We were going from house to house in Ramallah, looking for insurgents, but not really expecting to find any. It was more like a public relations mission. We had candy for the kids, that kind of thing. Shaking hands, making nice. It was a Shiite neighborhood, they were glad we were there. My guys went into a house, and I stayed outside in the lane playing kickball with some of the kids. Next thing, a bomb goes off. That's what I was told. I don't remember anything past playing kickball."

"Your guys. Were they good friends?"

"The best I'll ever have."

"Your wife left you while you were there."

He nodded. "In a way I can't blame her."

"Well, I can," she said.

He laughed. "Okay, you go ahead and blame her. I'm going swimming."

He left his shirt on the sand and ran into the sea, diving into the waves as they curled over his back. He swam so far his head looked like a buoy. When he came out of the water, he was breathing heavily, and his trunks were stuck to his legs. The skin around his eyes was unnaturally lined for a man of his age, as if the war had been etched into his face.

"I forgot how strong the undertow is here."

"It is," Helena said. "You have to watch the waves as you come out."

"Waves usually come in sets of seven, did you know that?"

"No, I didn't. I wonder why."

"Something to do with the wind."

She took off her sunglasses. "Do you ever feel alone? I mean completely alone? No, probably not, you have your father."

"There is nothing more lonely than being a sole survivor," he said.

Suddenly, she wanted their conversation to end. She couldn't feel sorry for both him and herself. She didn't have it to give.

The south point of the beach ended at a sliver of pebbled sand that was revealed only when the tide was very low. Though it was possible to get around the point, there was nothing but dense jungle on the other side. Guests were urged to swim directly in front of the resort where the water was clear of rocks and coral. Helena pounded up and down the mile of beach and swam within the limits. Out of boredom she rented a mask and snorkel and watched needlefish chase minnows. Idly, she paged through the book she'd brought, unable to concentrate. She'd often had a wonderful time alone at St. Jude, but all she could think of now was home.

"I feel as if I've left something undone," she told Daniel as they sat on the beach. "Like forgotten to turn off the stove. It's anxiety, I know. That's why I'm drinking so much. I never used to drink at lunch. Actually, I've been drinking pretty much all day."

"You don't have to," he said. "And you shouldn't drink if you're going to swim alone the way you do."

"Oh, I've been swimming in this water—"

"For years."

"Am I that much of a broken record?"

"We've talked a lot, is all. Just do me a favor and don't swim by yourself if you've had anything to drink."

"See, you are nice," she said. "Larry would never say something like that."

"From what you tell me Larry is a big baby. Why did you marry him?"

"Because he asked me to."

"That's not a very good reason."

"Good enough for me."

Daniel sighed and shook his head. "I'm going to go get Dad ready for lunch."

"May I eat with you?" Helena asked.

He looked surprised. "Of course."

Daniel brought his father to the hotel's restaurant on his arm. "This is Mrs. Temple," he said. "She's staying in the room next to ours."

"How do you do, Mr. Booker," Helena said. Mr. Booker mumbled a response and dipped his bald, freckled head.

"Dad was a general. People call him General Booker."

"It's a pleasure to meet you, General Booker."

Daniel helped him into his seat. They studied the menu together. Daniel ordered for his father and himself. Helena asked the waiter for a rum and orange juice. A breeze rattled the umbrella that shaded their table. Daniel and his father were comfortably silent. Helena sipped her drink.

"Lovely day," she said.

"Mrs. Temple said it's a lovely day," Daniel told his father. "Dad's deaf and he doesn't like his hearing aids. He says he hears static when he puts them in. "Isn't that right, Dad?" General Booker agreed in a quavering voice. The food came. Daniel cut up his father's meat, and handed him his water so the old man wouldn't have to reach for the glass. "Dad was at the Battle of the Bulge," he said.

"Really?" Helena searched her mind. "That was in Belgium?" The general nodded.

"He was awarded the Medal of Honor by President Truman. Let me do that for you, Dad." He speared some lettuce onto his father's fork and carefully placed the fork in his hand. Helena noticed that the food on Daniel's plate was untouched. He was making sure his father ate first.

"It's beautiful," she said.

"What is?"

"Your relationship."

Daniel didn't reply. His hair blew across his forehead, revealing a sudden line of pale scalp. At the end of the meal, he helped his father up. "If you wait for me, I'll go swimming with you," he said to Helena.

"Terrific," she said.

She walked down to her chaise, sat at the end of it. She waited for Daniel, but he didn't appear. Impatiently, she untied her beach wrap and ran into the sea. She swam to where the cerulean turned abruptly to indigo, then turned around and swam back to shore just as Daniel came down to the beach. He cupped his mouth with both hands and shouted something.

"What?" she shouted back. Then she was turned upside down by a wave and spun like a wheel beneath the churning water. A second wave slammed her into the sand; a third spat her onto the shore. As the wave sucked back, she went with it, and was caught and churned again. It was like being shaken up in a green bottle, she thought before she hit the shore once more. Stand up, she told herself. That was all she had to do. Stand up and walk out of the water. She let a fresh wave crash over her and pull her in again, dragging her through the shifting sand. Her muscles went slack as she let the undertow take her. It was a relief to stop fighting, so simple to let go.

Daniel grabbed her by her arms and dragged her onto the beach. Roughly, he turned her over and pulled her to her feet. "What the hell do you think you're doing? I told you to wait for me. You could have drowned."

"I wanted to drown." She brushed a sandy strand of hair from her eyes. "Suddenly it seemed like a good idea."

He slapped her so hard across the face that she fell back into the sand.

"My God," she cried. "You hit me!"

He squatted down beside her. "Death isn't a toy you play with. Death is real, you silly fool. You think your life is over because your husband left you? You don't get to decide whether to live or die."

She pressed both hands to her stinging cheek as he stood and walked away.

She woke the next morning wrapped in a wreck of sheets, empty minibar bottles, and a half-eaten 3 Musketeers surrounding her like ships on a stormy sea. Her head throbbed when she sat up; her mouth was so dry it was sticky. It would be a few minutes before her breakfast arrived, but stepping out onto the patio to wait for it, she knew she wouldn't be able to eat. She sat down and laid her cheek against the cool glass of the table. It still stung from Daniel's slap. Surely he would apologize today, and of course she would accept. She felt as sorry for him now as she did for herself—there was plenty of regret to share. She listened for the familiar sounds from next door, the clatter of cutlery and the general's mumble, but could only hear the crash and fizzle of the waves, the scrape of the palms, and the sing-song voice of a hotel maid delivering breakfast a few rooms away.

"Daniel?" she said. She didn't expect an answer; she could tell no one was there. She walked around the wall between their patios and peered through the glass door to his room. The curtain was drawn, but there was a small gap between them through which she could see two neatly made beds. Well, of course, she thought: military men. They would make their beds automatically.

"Ma'am?" A maid stood at the edge of the patio, holding a breakfast tray.

"My goodness!" Helena stepped away from the window. "You startled me. I was just looking for my friends."

"They checked out," the maid said. "Went off on the first boat."

Painfully, Helena nodded her head and stretched a false smile across her teeth. "Oh yes, of course! I'd forgotten."

She turned back to the window and saw herself reflected, and the uniformed maid behind her; and the beach; and the sea and sky joined at an invisible seam. A bruise of cloud cast a swift shadow on the water. She would be leaving soon, too.

Poor Bob

"DO YOU STILL LOVE ME?" I asked. I don't know why. It just popped
out as I sat there watching him die, a childish question from the
mouth of a grown woman. *Still. Still* presumed that he had loved
me at one time, but might not, had some reason to not love me
anymore. But I didn't presume he had loved me ever. In fact,
there were long periods in my life when I was convinced he didn't,
despite what people said. And funny enough, they said it quite
often: "Your father adores you, you know." I couldn't imagine where
they got their information. He was the least emotive person I knew,
unsentimental in the extreme, untouched by Christmas and babies
and weddings, ceremonies of any kind, an agnostic rather than an
atheist because, obviously, one never knew. He didn't believe in an
afterlife, so this was it, the end. Death was nigh and he was looking
forward to nothing, which made me feel sorry for him.

"Always have, always will," he said to the ceiling, his desiccated
profile cut like a coin against the sunlit curtain the nurses kept
drawn. I was embarrassed I'd asked the question, so the fact that
he didn't turn his head and look at me, or open his eyes at all, was
a relief because I wouldn't have known how to respond. Someone
else might have said, "I love you, too." Most people would have said
that. But if he was waiting for me to speak, he didn't wait long,

because a moment later he was quietly snoring, and I got up and left him alone.

The hallway seemed unnaturally bright compared to the dusk of my father's bedroom, every window a cacophony of glittering yellow light. My children's voices came from outdoors, where they were playing in the swimming pool.

I stepped out onto the patio, where my stepmother sat at a glass-topped table, keeping an eye on the girls for me and paging through a magazine. I'd left my Nikon on the table before I went inside; I picked it up and shot a picture of Jill, my eldest daughter, cannonballing into the water. I was a photographer in my real life, away from this place and the past.

"Well, they haven't drowned yet!" my stepmother said. She was trying hard to be cheerful, I knew, though I didn't see the point. Soon she would be a widow and there was nothing anyone could do about it. But she was a determinedly glass-half-full person, energetic and gregarious. My father had been ill for a long time, and she was undoubtedly starved of the social life they had once enjoyed. She shielded her eyes from the sun with the magazine. "They actually swim quite well."

The *actually* was a dig, or I felt it as such, as both my daughters still wore their baby fat and weren't interested in sports. We were all a little out of shape, including my husband, Thomas, but I was only self-conscious about it when I was around people who were obsessed with being fit. My stepmother was thin and muscular from her personal training at a gym, and though the day was blazing she wore tall boots and tight britches from her morning ride on her horse. She was my father's third wife, and the best of the two since my mother, because she genuinely cared about him. The one before had made him a cuckold by running off with a richer man. My father called her *the gold digger* after that, and certainly she was, but no more or less so than she had been when he'd chosen her for his wife. This one, the third one—her name was Marielle—was twenty years my father's junior, and though unquestionably a gold digger too, she thought my father was a brilliant man. "Which shows,"

Thomas said, "how stupid she is." I didn't think she was stupid, exactly, but I thought she didn't know much. *Lack-of-informationitis,"* was what I called her deficit, which made Thomas laugh every time.

My father's house, in the Virginia countryside, was surrounded by white-fenced fields. At one time he kept a lot of horses, but now there were only two. Colorful flower gardens bordered the house and the pool; twin rows of oaks canopied the long driveway that wound up from the road. There was a butter-colored barn and a stable, and the neighboring pasture was filled with black-and-white cows. An idyllic spot, I'd been married here. But I grew up from the age of eight, when my parents divorced, in a suburb of Richmond, where my mother was from, and went to boarding school outside of Washington. After college, I moved to New York City, and that was where I settled. I was only here now, in the shocking heat of July, because my father was near death. I brought the children along because he was their grandfather and it seemed like the right thing to do. But my father and Marielle had never been interested in the girls, and all the girls cared about were the horses and the pool and a litter of kittens that belonged to the cat in the barn. They were only seven and nine. I wondered if I should send them back to New York, but Thomas, who had stayed behind, didn't think I should.

"Why?" he said. "They're having fun. Let them enjoy your father's place one last time before Marielle absconds with the whole kaboodle."

I doubt my father would have told me that he was leaving everything he had to Marielle if she hadn't insisted he do so. I believe he would have preferred his lawyer tell me when he was already dead. I suppose he was expecting me to make a scene about it.

"Do what you want," was all I said. It was the unspoken truth that he always had.

"I can't leave Marielle destitute," he said, as if I'd suggested he should. "And this is her home, after all."

It was wintertime, and we were sitting by the fire in the den. Marielle was sitting with us, tensely chewing her lower lip. I guess she didn't trust my father to tell me unless she was there to make him. It couldn't be easy to break it to your only child that you're cutting her out of your will, especially as I had never been any trouble to him, and had always been friendly to Marielle. But he was sick then, and knew it, and Marielle would have been the one to see that he was properly cared for at home, which I admit I would not have done. She was greedy and he was terrified: there was no more to it than that.

Perhaps Marielle really was stupid, because she clearly expected us to continue being friendly despite all she'd caused me to lose. But to be hateful to her seemed like a waste of energy; it was more fun to be hateful about her.

I took a few more pictures of the girls playing in the pool, then turned my camera on Marielle. She was a beautiful woman, even though she was deep into her fifties, with thick brown hair cut in a girlish bob and a light tan that she managed to maintain year round.

"Oh no, don't, I'm a sight," she said, holding the magazine in front of her face. The magazine was *Vogue* and Michelle Obama was on the cover. Marielle had the most offensive bumper sticker I'd ever seen on her car that read, LET'S PUT THE WHITE BACK INTO THE WHITE HOUSE. I'd attempted to tear it off several times. The way she held the magazine placed Michelle Obama's face squarely on her neck. I got in several shots before she put the magazine down.

"How is your daddy, do you think?" she asked.

"Well, he could talk," I said.

"Oh! That's wonderful!" She smiled. "What did he say?"

"He said he was thirsty," I lied. She looked concerned. But my father had a phalanx of nurses that came and went in shifts and saw to his smallest needs. The one who was "on" at the moment had passed me as I left his room, reeking of the cigarette she'd smoked during the break I'd given her by sitting with him. "Flavia is in there," I said.

"Oh, Flavia." Marielle wrinkled her nose. "Do you know what I pay her and the others? Forty dollars an hour! It's an outrage, really, but I couldn't get anyone for less."

So the money was already hers in her mind. I was surprised she was such a skinflint, but of course she wouldn't have had any idea what a fair wage was now, or what it cost most people to live. Before she'd married my father, she was a manager at a local restaurant; prior to that, she'd lived in Jamaica—with a man who supported her, I gathered, because no occupation during those years had ever been mentioned. Four barely visible holes curved from her left earlobe up the edge of her ear. She'd removed the little gold hoops that hung from the holes when she took up with my father, who hadn't liked them. I wondered if she would put the hoops back in after he was gone. A long time ago she'd been married to her high school sweetheart.

"He was a loser," she always said about him, and I didn't doubt it because the son they'd had together was the most pathetic person I had ever met. Hating him was worth my energy, because when Marielle died, my father's money, the farm, the house and everything in it, would go not to me, not to my beautiful girls, but to this undeserving moron who lived in a trailer behind the stable and fed the horses for his keep at the age of thirty-five. Thomas liked to say he was retarded, but he wasn't in the least. He was wily and shiftless and recognized a good thing when he saw it. As far as I knew, he'd never had a job. My father always referred to him as *Poor Bob*, which irritated me, and doubtless Marielle, too. He wouldn't be poor much longer.

"How's Bob?" I said, because I was thinking about him. I didn't care how he was.

"Oh, he's terribly broken up about your father," Marielle said.

"I bet."

"What's that supposed to mean?"

"What is what supposed to mean?" I turned my camera on the girls again. "Great, Jill!" I called as she cannonballed for the umpteenth time. Her little sister Jenny sat at the edge of the pool, reflections from the water dancing across her face. They were both getting sunburnt on their shoulders and noses, but they were dark-haired, like me, and olive-skinned, and by tomorrow the pink would be brown.

"When you said 'I bet,'" Marielle persisted. "About Bob."

"Hmm? What do you bet about Bob?" I focused the camera on her face. "Gosh, you look pretty today."

"Oh, no I don't. I'm a wreck and you know it." She touched her hair and looked away so I wouldn't see the tears in her eyes.

Dusk came late and lasted a long time; the sky was still light when I put my daughters to bed. I left the house and walked up to the highest pasture, where I looked down on my father's domain. The long white house and the blue rectangle of the pool, the stable and the big yellow barn: in the photo I snapped from the darkening distance it looked like a child's notion of a farm. I noticed that Bob was late collecting the horses from the field. As if he had anything else to do. I walked down to where they stood by the gate, patiently waiting to be brought in, and taking each by her halter, I led them out of the pasture and into the stable yard. They were gentle mares and easily led, one chestnut and the other a bay. I put the bay into her stall and tied the chestnut to a fencepost while I went to the tack room for a bridle.

"Hey, pretty girl," I murmured as I slipped the bridle over her head and settled the reins on her withers. The sun had dropped behind the hills but I could see what I was doing by the light I'd left on when I went into the tack room for the bridle. Clicking my tongue, I led the horse to the mounting block and swung my leg over her bare back with nearly painless agility. I pressed my knees to her flanks, tugged the reins, and she obliged by turning around. It's been said that smell, more than any other sense, is the strongest memory trigger. As I leaned into the mare's neck and breathed her warm scent, I was reminded of a time so sweet and abandoned that I closed my eyes and simply lay there with my nose against her rough mane. I'd had a pony when I was a child, before my parents divorced. Cupcake was the name I gave him, and I remembered loving him the way people love dogs. I didn't know the name of the mare I was riding, but she tolerated my displaced affection as if strangers lay on her neck every day.

"The fuck you doin'?"

He had put on a lot of weight since the last time I saw him, his stomach now shadowed his belt, and lost enough hair that the tack room light glanced bright off the top of his head. His jeans puddled around his sneakers, frayed white where they dragged at the heels, and his T-shirt looked like it had been wiped with a grimy hand. That he had lost his bottom right incisor completed the picture. I itched to take a photo, but I'd left my camera on the fencepost.

"Bob," I said. "Always a pleasure."

"Get off Mom's horse," he said.

"Bob, this is my father's horse. I can ride her if I want to." I could see he wasn't listening, or understanding, and then I realized he was very drunk.

"S'Mom's," he said, and grabbed for the bridle. The horse abruptly shied away from him and I nearly fell off of her. Wrapping a hank of her mane around my hand, I held on tight as the mare backed away from Bob. Without a saddle, my seat was precarious, and though Bob was clumsy with liquor, I thought he wasn't beyond doing damage to me or the horse, or both.

"Okay, Bob," I said in a placating voice. "Just let me dismount. Okay?"

As I turned the mare toward the mounting block, she suddenly bucked hard. I lost my grip on her mane and fell into the dust. Instinctively, I rolled away from her prancing hooves and lay still until she calmed. I'd fallen on my side and lost my breath, but other than a dull pain in my ribs, I thought I was okay. I got up slowly, stiff as an old woman. Cooing sweet words, I walked over to her and carefully took her by her bridle, but she was as docile now as she was before, and went obediently into her stall. Night had truly fallen and I felt in a hurry to get back to the girls. I was on my way to retrieve my camera when I discovered Bob passed out on the ground.

"Bob!" I called. "Get up and go home!" I walked over to him and squatted down. He smelled strongly of alcohol and sweat. His eyelids were purple and deeply creased; broken blood vessels blushed over his nose and cheeks. His mouth hung open, showing the black gap in his teeth. I shook his shoulder and tried to heave him up, but he was as heavy as a sack of cement, so I let him drop, dust flying where he fell. There was obviously something wrong with him. I had to look hard to understand what it was. In the light of the tack room I finally saw that the mare had kicked in his left temple when she bucked out with her hooves. There was a depression between his eye and ear where the bone under the skin had been crushed.

I didn't try to help him. He was beyond help, anyway. His wound was so subtle he appeared to be asleep, and like most sleeping beings, innocent. I walked out of the stable yard and up the dark pasture, through the already dampening grass, and entered the house by the front door, which nobody ever used.

When I checked on the girls, I found Jenny awake and asking for a glass of water. I took her to the bathroom, then led her back to her room, which had been mine when I was her age.

"Mommy? Is that you?" she said as we walked down the hall.

I looked at the painting she was pointing to, an oil of me at seventeen. My father had asked a local artist to paint my portrait before I went away to college. I remembered being ordered not to move as I sat in the artist's studio, and in the end not liking the painting because he hadn't made me look pretty. My skin was muddy, and the background dashed off; my hair was a dark mass lacking any lights. Nevertheless, he had captured me: my hooded brown eyes and dissatisfied mouth, the way I tended to turn my head to the right. I saw that now for the first time, youthful vanity put aside. Though I had passed the portrait countless times, I was startled now by my guileless young self.

After I tucked Jenny back into bed, I went to see my father. The nurse sat in a chair outside his bedroom, reading a paperback.

"She's in there," she said, meaning Marielle. "He's near the end. I told her so."

"How near?" I said.

She shook her head. "No more than a day. He's sleeping. I gave him a shot of morphine. He won't wake up."

I opened the door. Marielle was sitting in a straight-backed chair close beside my father's bed. I walked up behind her and put my hand on her shoulder.

"You're tired," I said. "Let me sit with him. You go lie down. I'll come get you if anything changes."

"Your daddy is dying," she said.

I held her hand as she stood up. I wondered if she smelled the stable on me, but she would have said so if she did.

"Go on now. I'm right here."

"I am awfully tired," she said.

I sat down in the chair and took up my vigil. It wasn't so late, only about ten o'clock, but I was prepared to be there all night. My father's face was waxy pale except for the pinkish tip of his nose, as if all the life left in his body had gathered in that one spot. The morphine had done its job; he was insensible to my presence. But I was going to talk to him, anyway. I had something I wanted to say.

"You were a terrible father to me," I said. "I never knew how bad until Thomas and I became parents and I saw how a good father behaves. My daughters, your granddaughters, will have something I never had, the knowledge that no one in the world is more important to their father. It's a miracle to me. I'm lucky, so lucky. I escaped being married to a man like you. Isn't that what girls do? Marry men like their fathers? Well, I didn't, and I can only thank God for that, because I wouldn't have known any better."

I sat back and was quiet. What a coward I was, speaking my mind to him when he couldn't possibly hear me. There was no purpose to what I was doing.

"Bob is dead," I said after a while. "I didn't kill him, but I'm not sorry."

The sky was pink when I woke. I had slept sitting up all night. I started and reached for my father's wrist. I felt the warmth of his skin, and heard his breathing, even and calm. I sat until dawn grew into day before I went to wake Marielle.

"Daddy's still sleeping," I told her.

"It's another beautiful day," she said. "Just like yesterday. It's strange, isn't it? How bad things can happen on the prettiest days."

"As if the weather is mocking you," I said.

"It should be raining today. And cold."

I thought of Bob waiting in the stable yard, the rising sun pulling away the blanket of night that he'd slept under undisturbed. Marielle would find him when she went for her morning ride. My father would die that day. The girls and I would go home to Thomas. There would be all sorts of weather to come.

THE NARROW RIM

HARLAN DIDN'T HONESTLY CARE what was in the deviled eggs, it wasn't as if he planned on making any, but it was something to talk to the hostess of the party about while he waited for a drink at the bar. This was not his crowd. He didn't know anyone but Stan, the birthday boy, who was a colleague from a former job.

"They're delicious," he said, wiping his mouth on a cocktail napkin.

"Miracle Whip is the secret ingredient," the hostess said. "Disgusting, I know, but that's what makes them so creamy."

"I have nothing against Miracle Whip." He didn't even know what it was. The hostess was Stan's fiancé. She was attractive without being pretty, a vigorous-looking blond. She wore a spangled black dress and a big diamond ring. He was dying for a drink. He tried to get the bartender's attention, but the guy was pouring glasses of Chardonnay for three chattering, middle-aged women. In the left inside pocket of his suit jacket were four Oxycodone tablets; he considered going to the bathroom and swallowing a couple. Finally, the bartender handed him a martini. "Oh, great," he said with relief.

The party was being held in a large, open loft. Candles flickered everywhere, creating a shadowy, ecclesiastical aura. He turned back to the fiancé, but she'd taken the opportunity to move on in the half-second he looked away. He hoped he hadn't bored her, or was boring in general tonight, because he wanted to pick up a woman.

He spotted a few young lovelies here and there, and a far larger number of women milling around who were too old, or too fat, or otherwise unappealing. He was looking for someone in between, like Stan's fiancé. What did she see in him? Stan was the kind of guy who knew a little about a lot of things, always spouting inane facts in a fatuous blah-blah voice. He wasn't handsome, either. But women liked to fall in love and get married, and, if possible, have children, and he thought it was probably obvious that he wasn't interested in any of that. He had an ounce of really good weed at home that he intended to smoke with whoever he picked up. That was the type of woman he wanted, one who appreciated the occasional toke. He drained his martini, cadged another, and shouldered into the crowd.

He always slept soundly on cloudy mornings, and was shocked into consciousness by the alarm. He opened his eyes to a hangover and what appeared to be a child in his bed. She turned over and looked at him, a calm, green-eyed stare.

"Jesus Christ, how old are you?"

"Twenty-three," she said. "I told you already. You were super fucked up last night."

"Not too fucked up," he said hopefully.

She smiled. "You were able to do it, if that's what you're wondering. You came, I came, it was okay. You said you loved me, but don't worry, I didn't believe you."

She got up and walked to the bathroom, unashamedly naked. And for good reason, Harlan thought. There were twin dimples above her heart-shaped ass; hair the color of bourbon nearly reached her tiny waist. He had zero memory of whatever he did or said to lure her into his bed.

"So, we met at the party? How do you know Stan?"

"He's my boss," she called from the bathroom. "Another thing I told you last night. Don't you remember anything? Do you usually get so plowed?"

"I remember your name is Dahlia." He felt like he'd won a prize.

She came to the bathroom door. "It's Deborah, actually." She watched his face. "No, I'm just playing with you. It is Dahlia. That was fantastic weed, by the way. Can I have the name of your dealer?" She went back into the bathroom, and he heard the hiss of the shower.

He remembered it was Saturday; he'd forgotten to turn off the alarm. He opened the bedside table drawer, took out a silver pill box, chewed an Oxy and waited for his hangover to wane, dozing until he heard her get out of the shower.

"Don't go," he said when she came out of the bathroom. "Let's do something. I'll take you to brunch, we can go to the zoo."

"The zoo?"

"As an example."

"I wouldn't mind getting high again."

"Whatever you want."

She looked at him with narrowed eyes. "I didn't take you for a guy who'd be friendly the morning after. I hope you don't send me flowers. I would have left earlier but I overslept. I can't stand brunch. I can't even stand the word."

"Neither can I. The weed is in the living room. I'll get it."

"Actually." She reached into her purse, a big brown leather sack, and took out one of his joints. She shrugged. "A parting gift. But since we're not parting." Fishing around in the bag again, she produced a tiny pink lighter. She sat on the bed, lit the joint, and handed it over to Harlan.

"I'm not a morning-after guy, usually. It's rare that I have sex with anyone I want to stay over. No one like you, anyway."

"I know, I'm so beautiful," she said in a bored voice. "You can't believe your luck. You said all that last night, too, before you told me you loved me."

Harlan grimaced. "I made a fool out of myself."

"Not at all, you were sweet. I wouldn't be here if I didn't like you. But don't get any ideas. I don't *like* like you. You just seem like a cool guy. A little older than I prefer, but whatever. Thirty-five-year-old guys wearing business suits don't usually have superior weed and a lifetime supply of Oxy."

"I have a bum shoulder," he said. "Chronic pain."

"Uh huh. Tell me another."

"That could be true."

"But it's not."

She lay back on the pillows and stretched out a slim leg. Her eyelids fluttered as she inhaled. The bedroom seemed as gray as the day, soft and undemanding. The street below was quiet. Harlan gazed out the window at a plastic grocery bag caught in a bare tree being punched here and there by a breeze. It was beautiful, he thought, sculptural, a different shape with every gust. He wondered if Dahlia would have sex with him again. He'd like to remember it this time.

"Can I have your number?"

"What for?" She waved away a floating island of smoke.

"So I can call you."

"Why?"

He sucked on the joint and spoke in a choked voice. "For a date. I want to take you out. To a restaurant, or a movie. Like that."

She turned to him, her face serious. There was a saddle of pale freckles across her nose.

"Now, listen. I know how you thirty-something guys are, time is ticking away and you're looking for someone to have a family with." She said *family* as if it tasted bad. "If that's your deal, then no, you can't have my number. I loathe that kind of crap."

"What kind of crap?" Harlan said, fascinated.

"Love, marriage, the baby carriage. It's just not for me, okay?"

"Okay! Fantastic!" He handed the joint back to her. It was so burnt down he could barely hold it. She took it between her long fingernails and inhaled, igniting the final ember.

"You are precisely the woman of my dreams," he said.

"Oh, spare me. There is no such thing."

He asked her to meet him at his favorite restaurant, a leather banquet and dark wood kind of place that always seemed smoky even though nobody smoked. She was late, and by the time she came in he had downed an Oxy and two shots of tequila. He sat facing the door because he wanted to see her before she saw him. She wore a smart little pants suit and an open-necked shirt. Her heels were absurdly high.

"How do you walk in those?"

"In what?" She sat down. "Can I have a manhattan? I've been thinking about a manhattan."

"Tough day?"

She stared at him. "No. We are not going to do that. We are not going to talk about our jobs and our favorite movies and where we hope to be in five years. This is why I don't go on dates, the conversation is excruciating. Tell me the weirdest thing you ever did."

"My sister had this big aquarium full of fish." He spoke so fast the words tumbled into each other. "Every now and then, I would take one out and flush it down the toilet. She didn't usually notice until a couple of days later, and then she would freak out. 'Where is my zebrafish,' or whatever. Tropical fish are expensive, and my parents would have to replace them. Finally they got fed up and made her get rid of the aquarium. By that time she had about one fish left. They thought the fish were eating each other. They never suspected me."

Dahlia laughed, delighted. "So weird! Why did you do it?"

"To drive her crazy. Which it did. She was fourteen, I was nine."

"That is a perfect story." She leaned across the table and kissed him on the mouth. She smelled of perfume and body odor.

Though they saw each other almost every night, neither would have said they were dating. She liked to tie him up and ride him. She gave blowjobs like a pro. She skirted the edge of kinky. "I do not do anal," he insisted. She laughed and called him a prude. It was easy not to know each other through the screen of sex and weed.

"Where did you come from?" he asked in wonder.

"You mean originally? Chicago. Who is the grossest person you've ever known?"

"My freshman roommate," he said immediately. She was impatient; thirty seconds of thought was too long. He'd come to enjoy the challenge of thinking fast while stoned. "He used to pick his nose and wipe the snot on the front of his shirt. He picked his nose a lot, he had some sort of sinus problem, so by the end of the day his shirt would be a minefield of boogers."

"No way!" She fell back onto the bed, her hair fanning around her head. "That is truly, truly gross."

He opened his bedside table drawer and took out the silver pillbox.

"How many of those do you take a day?"

"I don't know. Five or six, I guess."

"Where do you get them?"

"Various sources. There's a place called The Pain Center, downtown. I really did break my scapula about four years ago. I go in and tell them it's acting up and they give me whatever I want. And I have a college friend who's a dermatologist. He's cool, I can get prescriptions from him. The guy I get my weed from sells it, too. He's who I've been buying it from lately, though he's way more expensive than the pharmacy."

"So, you're addicted."

He frowned at her. "What? No. Why would you say that?"

She rolled over onto her stomach and propped herself up on her elbows. Idly, she scissored her legs. "Six Oxys a day is not recreational, Harlan. I'm just stating a fact. I'm not saying I give a damn."

Harlan put the box away unopened. He had thought there wasn't anything she could say or do that wouldn't excite him. "Well, aren't we judgmental all of a sudden."

"I just told you I don't care."

"I don't *need* to take them, I *like* to."

She shrugged. "Okay."

"You don't believe me."

"Of course not. But it doesn't matter what I believe. It's your Oxy, it's your life. Everybody has their thing."

He rasped the stubble on his jaw with his palm. A balloon expanded in his throat. Easily, he could have struck her, twisted her arm, blackened her knowing green eyes. He scared himself, thinking this: he had never laid his hands on a woman for any reason that wasn't benign. Thinking wasn't doing, he told himself, and yet thought was a precipice, the narrow rim of the act. He had been raised to be a gentleman. His parents were loving and kind.

"Enough of it, then. I quit."

Dahlia sat up on her knees. "Whoa, Harlan. That is not a good idea. You've been taking those pills for four years. If you quit cold turkey you'll get really sick."

"Cold turkey," he scoffed. "What a stupid expression."

"No, really. You have to do it gradually."

"Your concern is adorable. Makes me think you have a thing for me."

"Well, think again," she said. "Don't do it for me."

"No, not for you," he said.

They shared a joint. Dahlia fell asleep. He opened the drawer, took a final Oxy from the box, and chased it down with the dregs of a martini before turning out the light.

Harlan was popular at work, thought of as a mellow and humorous guy, and co-workers gathering in his office wasn't unusual, shooting the breeze and wasting time. So, the morning after he quit taking Oxy, after he told his assistant that she was a goddamn idiot, word that something was "wrong with Harlan" spread through the cubicles like an odor.

Gerald, who worked in the office next to Harlan's, toed the jamb of Harlan's door. He jingled the change in his pocket. "I hear Sarah is pretty upset, Harlan. Just thought you should know."

Harlan glanced up from his computer. He was trying to write the first sentence of a memo. He kept forgetting what the memo was about and having to refer to the subject line, yet ten seconds later there he would be again, mindlessly studying the blinking cursor. Gerald looked like a photograph that had been fogged around the edges.

"What are you talking about," he said impatiently. "I haven't seen Sarah all day."

"That's because you were shitty to her."

The noise Gerald made floated across the room and finally reached him as words. He sat back. "Huh?"

"Well, that's the rumor. What did you say to her?"

The memory arrived like a punch. "Right. Never mind. I'll talk to her."

"Good idea," Gerald said. Then he disappeared as if he'd never been there, the conversation a dream. Harlan looked at the time. Six twenty-two. Sarah would have gone home. The memo remained an empty screen. He counted backward from midnight. Eighteen hours and twenty-two minutes.

Dahlia was waiting for him at the bar. She sat on a stool, dangling a spike-heeled shoe from one foot and staring at the wall of bottles with her chin in her hand. Her hair was up in a complicated new twist.

"Oh, good," she said as he sat down. "I'm bored to death. I've been here for half an hour."

"Why? Am I late? What time is it?"

"Chill out!" She laughed at him. "I'm early."

He ordered two shots of tequila and drank them one after the other, flashing two fingers at the bartender again. He wiped the back of his hand across his sweaty forehead. He saw Dahlia watching him out of the corner of his eye. Violence swelled in him a second time. He imagined slapping her off the stool, kicking her pretty head.

"Thirsty?" she said.

"So?"

"Just that. An observation."

The tequila sank in. He cracked his neck. For propriety's sake he would have to wait a little while before ordering another round. "I was shitty to my assistant today."

"Oh, too bad," Dahlia said.

"Well, I wish I hadn't been. She's a nice woman."

"She'll get over it. What was the worst vacation you ever took?"

He rubbed his eyes. He didn't have to think about it because it was the last vacation he'd taken. "Spain, three years ago. I had a couple of pitchers of sangria at a flamenco place and thought, oh, come on, anyone can stomp around with their hands on their hips. So I climbed up on stage and joined the dancers, and at first everyone thought it was funny. I felt like Lucille Ball or something, I was having a good time. But after a few minutes the audience started booing, and the maître d' came over and asked me to get off the stage. I told him to fuck off. So then a bunch of waiters pulled me off and someone called the police. Or maybe the police were already there. It was confusing. Anyway, long story short, I ended up spending the night in a stinking Spanish jail with a couple of gypsy pickpockets. You would not have believed how filthy those guys were. They were actually crusty."

"That's awful!" Dahlia said. "Seriously? Are you kidding?"

Harlan shook his head no and instantly regretted it. It felt like a hacky sack was being kicked around in there. "They let me out in time to fly home. The woman I had been traveling with was already gone. I was in love with her, in case you want to hear about that. No, of course you don't." He gave the waiter the sign for two more.

Dahlia rested her elbows on the bar and looked at him.

"That's six shots in less than half an hour," she said as the bartender put down his drinks.

"Yes, it is. Since when were you a teetotaler?"

She raised her hands in surrender. "Drink up."

"Oh, thanks so much."

"Let's go to your place and smoke some weed. Let's fuck. Let's do something."

"Have you always been so easily bored? Were you one of those ADHD children? Special ed? That's probably why you like sex so much, no mental acuity necessary." An electric prod drove through the left side of his head. He smacked his hand against his eye. Dahlia's face briefly multiplied. "Shit, I've got a horrible headache."

"Serves you right for being such a dick."

"You are an empty can, you know that?" he said. "Who the hell are you, anyway? I don't even know your middle name."

"It's Rose," she said. "You can screw yourself from now on."

She gave the bartender a credit card and signed off on the bill. Her shoulder brushed against his. Body odor and perfume: her uniquely sexy scent.

"Your hands are shaking," she said as she put on her coat.

It wasn't his hands that were shaking so much as his arms. They felt like rubber hoses. *I am dying*, he thought, or said. "Did I just say something?" he asked her, but she appeared not to have heard.

Darkness so dense it had texture, shards of black upon black, a pixelated picture of nothing, what being dead must be like. Slowly, eventually, Harlan realized that the freezing surface beneath him was tile. He found the rim of a bathtub and pulled himself to his knees, then felt his way to a threshold, a door, a knob, and finally his bedroom, where the windows glowed yellow with the city at night. Grabbing the doorjamb for ballast, he snapped on the bathroom light. Vomit everywhere. On the floor, in the sink, on the toilet seat, and in the tub, spattered on his shirtfront and tie. A wide stain darkened the crotch of his trousers and felt damp against his thighs. He remembered being very drunk and getting into a cab. He understood that the vomit was his, and only he could have wet himself.

"Dahlia?" he called. He both wanted her and didn't. In any case, she wasn't there. He was tapped out of ways to delight her; he had no more stories to tell. "What's the stupidest thing you ever did?" she once asked. He couldn't remember what he said, but it must have been difficult to choose a single incident, he'd been stupid every day for so long.

He shimmied out of his pants and gingerly shucked his shirt. Naked, he limped to the bed. Muscles he never knew about throbbed; his headache settled into the back of his head. Twenty-four hours and twelve minutes. It was the longest he'd gone since three years before, when he'd almost made it through two days. That time, too, he'd quit because of a girl—no, *for* a girl. He closed his eyes against the thought of her. "Fuck you," he told himself. She had brought him aspirin and water, and tried to make him eat; she lay in bed with him and held him while he cried—crying, too, because what hurt him hurt her, never letting him go. But she did go; she had to, just for an hour. There was food to be bought, more aspirin and water. She returned to find him in a fulsome haze, having taken three Oxys from a hidden stash the minute she walked out the door.

Wrapping his arms around himself, he felt his heart skip and whirr. He wouldn't be surprised if a hummingbird flew out of his mouth, or a whole flock of them, why not? He threw back the covers, suddenly burning, and went to find some Tylenol in the medicine cabinet. There was a crust of vomit at the corner of his mouth, storm cloud of a bruise on his chin. The bristles on his jaw were going gray, and so was his clipped, dark hair. By now, he would have had a couple of babies and a house outside the city. That was their plan, anyway. She wasn't ambitious for a big career; family was her thing. She had been an only child. Both their parents were divorced.

"That will never happen to us," she'd said, and he agreed, impossible.

"I can't imagine not being with you." He thought he saw the future.

He broke his scapula during a ski trip. He banged down hard on the ice and couldn't get up, in too much pain to move. She knelt beside him until the ski patrol came and skied with them down to the lodge. At the hospital he was given Demerol. He had never felt anything as good. It was better than sex, he told her. She laughed and said, "Oh, great! We better get you out of here." He was sent home with a prescription for Percocet, and that was the beginning of their end.

The numbers on the cable box read 12:31. The night lay before him like a horizonless plain; he knew he wouldn't sleep. He stared at the grid on the walls cast by the streetlight through the window. Occasionally he would google her to see if she'd gotten married. When nothing came up, his relief was so profound that tears would come to his eyes. She wasn't pretty, but she made everyone laugh, and laughed at herself; she didn't have a vain bone in her body. She was a pixie, a gamine, playful as a child. But she knew what she wanted, and it wasn't him.

"When did you decide to become an asshole?" she'd asked him. "At what point did you give up on everything good about yourself?" They'd been walking in the maze at the Alcazar gardens in Seville on an achingly blue afternoon. She was two hedges away, only her head and shoulders visible. He was high on Oxy and wearing sunglasses so she wouldn't see his eyes. The question came out of nowhere. They'd been admiring the palace and gardens, the beautifully painted tiles. "Where is that smart, sweet, lovely man? Tell me, Harlan. Will I ever see him again?"

"I'm right here," he said. It was all he had. He'd looked down at himself, at the gravel path, at his jeans and his sneakers with the boomerangs on their sides. When he looked up, she was gone. Forever, it turned out, but he didn't know that then.

As cold now as he had been hot before, his skin beginning to itch, he rolled himself into a ball like a defended animal and tucked his hands between his knees. There were thirty-two pills in his bedside drawer, ample means to erase his misery. "I'm clean," he imagined telling her. She would be happy for him. He watched the still shadows on the ceiling and walls, so different than the shadows of the sun.

Indoor Voice

Once a month, Jenna saw her psychopharmacologist, Dr. Pryzansky. For fifteen minutes, she told him how she felt and what she'd been doing, and then he wrote out her prescriptions and presented them to her in a neat little fan. Though she had been seeing him for a year, she still thought of him as "new," and suspected he felt the same way because he sometimes forgot who she was. Once he asked her how her children were, and she had to remind him she didn't have any, and another time he asked if she enjoyed her vacation when she hadn't been anywhere. It was lovely, she told him to spare them both the awkwardness. So relaxing, I didn't want to come back. Then just for the hell of it, she went on to describe a vacation in Bermuda a customer once described to her. She wondered if the patient Pryzansky was thinking of had gone on a different kind of trip, had taken a cruise to Alaska, or bicycled through the South of France, but he listened impassively to her description of pink beaches and turquoise water until their time ran out. For a moment she thought of telling him the truth: I'm just shitting you, Pryzansky, I've never been to Bermuda. But that would make her seem crazy, manic, and who knew how he would react. The last thing she needed was for him to take an interest and start screwing around with her meds. The doctor she saw before Pryzansky had died of a stroke, and through some arrangement she never fully understood, Pryzansky had inherited his patients.

Lying about the vacation had been more entertaining than talking about herself, so the next time Pryzansky mistook her for another patient and asked if she'd gotten that promotion, she told him with feigned pride that she was a vice president now, and making double her former salary. The look on his face made her think he'd realized his mistake, but it turned out he was only surprised that she had gotten such a large raise. He had a point; people were losing their jobs every day. She decided to say that she worked for a chain of funeral homes.

"People pass away regardless of the economy. Of course, their loved ones aren't springing for the top-of-the-line caskets anymore, but fortunately that's not my division. I'm in Remains, Vice President of Cremation. It's a tough job, long hours, but, as you are no doubt aware, the perpetual abundance of human remains is an undeniable reality." She leaned forward as if to confide a secret. "Death is recession-proof, Doctor."

"I guess so," Pryzansky said, and took out his prescription pad.

In her real life, Jenna was a waitress at an expensive restaurant that specialized in childhood foods. Five nights a week, she served nostalgic adults grilled cheese sandwiches and chocolate pudding. At one time she had been an actor who supported herself by waiting tables, but after years of rarely getting any acting jobs and waiting on ever more tables, she now thought of herself as a waitress who used to be an actor. She hadn't been much of an actor, but she was an efficient and popular waitress; she made enough money in tips to live alone in a small one-bedroom apartment. She didn't care what she did for a living, as long as it paid the bills, because she felt lucky to be alive.

Six years before, she almost succeeded in killing herself by putting a plastic bag over her head and cutting her wrists with an X-acto blade. "You were serious," the doctor in the psych ward had said, almost in admiration. Waking up alive had been an astonishing relief at first. She could not fathom what made her do it. Then the suffocating gray veil that obscured the future wrapped itself around her once more, and she felt the old craving to destroy herself. "Why?" her mother asked repeatedly. She could not put her feelings into words. The only thing she knew was that she desperately needed to die.

"No, you don't," the doctor told her, as if she'd said she needed an elephant. She was given a spectrum of pills that made her feel nauseated and dizzy, then a new combination that didn't, and was released from the hospital thirty days later into an entirely different world than the one she had attempted to leave.

She told the guy she was dating about lying to Pryzansky because she thought it would make him laugh. He did laugh, they both did, but then he said, "You should really find a better shrink, Jenna. This joker sounds like an idiot."

"I don't pay him to think, I pay him to write my prescriptions."

"Well, now he thinks you work for a funeral home."

"A *chain* of funeral homes," she corrected, and they laughed about it again.

The guy, Brad, was a successful actor. He was Ken-doll handsome and did a lot of commercials, which made it possible for him to take on theatrical roles. On her nights off from the restaurant, Jenna would go to whatever play he was in and admire him from the mezzanine. "Isn't he a wonderful actor?" she would say to the person sitting next to her. "Don't you think he's handsome?" It thrilled her to hear strangers agree. Brad knew that Jenna had been an actor once, and thought she should try it again.

"You're beautiful," he said, twirling her long red hair around his index finger. "You gave up on yourself too soon."

"You don't know what giving up on yourself is," she said. She had an irrational fear that if she went back to acting she would want to kill herself again, as if the one thing had led to the other, both entwined in the veil of gray. She knew this wasn't true. She told Brad she was a mediocre actor. "It's exhausting trying to be better than you are, trying to believe in this person who really isn't you at all."

"But that's acting," Brad said. "Pretending you're someone else."

"I said believe in, not pretend." But she could see he didn't understand. She marveled at his simplicity. He was solid, indestructible; he had been the king of his senior prom. He would give her indestructible babies who would be exactly like him. She had been told by her doctor before Pryzansky that having her own children would be unwise. She would have to cycle off her medications to avoid damaging the fetus, and there was a genetic possibility that the child would share her illness. But she could not imagine her defective genes prevailing over Brad's solid and healthy ones, and she had found out from the Internet that only two of her medications were strictly contraindicated during pregnancy. Two out of four. She could deal with that. Nine months wasn't such a long time.

"I'm in love," she told Pryzansky. He asked her with whom.

"Whom?" she said. *Whom?* What a priggish word. She changed her mind. Her love for Brad was none of his business.

"Yes," Pryzansky said, a little impatiently. "With whom are you in love?"

"I am in love with a female impersonator," she said. "Oh, I know what you're thinking, and no, he's not gay. Everybody assumes that. He's quite virile, actually. I mean in bed. Let's just say he's ample." She paused to see Pryzansky's reaction. He reached up and lightly touched his comb-over, which was greasy and complex, the hair piled up from both one side and the back. She wondered if he believed this hairdo disguised the fact that he was bald, and if he cared so much, why didn't he get plugs or a weave. "Lon—that's his name, Lon—does all sorts of impersonations, but his specialty is Cher. He wears this long black wig and sings, *Babe, I got you, babe.*" She stood up and swung her long hair in imitation of Cher while holding an invisible microphone to her mouth. "He also does Madonna. *Like a Virgin,*" she sang, jutting her hips. *"Touched for the ve-ry first time.* Early Madonna, of course. Late Madonna is a bore."

She sat down again and crossed her thin legs, hooking one around the other. "Anyway, I went to his show with a mutual friend and we were invited backstage." She rolled her eyes and giggled. "It was love at first sight. I mean, even though he still had his wig and makeup on, I was irresistibly attracted to him. It was weird, though, to hear this deep voice come out of him when he said hello. He sounds like James Earl Jones. Then the three of us went out for a drink, and after that, since he and I both live downtown, we shared a cab and made out the whole ride. Then he came back to my place and we humped like monkeys."

"Well," Pryzansky said. He picked up his pad and wrote out her prescriptions. "Here you go. See you next time."

She told Brad about it and they laughed until they cried. "It was the first thing I thought of, isn't that weird? I made up a whole story."

"And you say you're a bad actor," he said.

"It was fun. I don't know if he believed me or not. I doubt he was paying attention, to tell you the truth."

"Then he missed a good show," Brad said.

She began to think about going back to acting. She took a class where she did basic exercises such as imagining she was a tree, then another where she sat at a table with other actors and read dramatically from famous plays. A friend of Brad's produced a showcase in which she played a drunken prostitute, her hair piled messily on top of her head and a cigarette dangling from her lip. The cigarette had been her idea. Emboldened, she auditioned for a stage play, and won the part of the waitress.

"Of course I got the part, I *am* a waitress," she said when Brad insisted on celebrating. It was a tiny production in a makeshift theater on the Lower East Side; the only people who came to see it were the families and friends of the actors. She knew it was the best she could expect. At thirty-three, her looks were on the wane. Her once brilliant blue eyes looked sleepy and faded, and there was a geyser of creases above the bridge of her nose. If she had any ambition, these signs of aging would have bothered her, but she still associated acting with sadness, and the bleak little Lower East Side production had made her feel sorry for everyone involved.

Brad was playing Macbeth on Broadway. He was breathtaking, Jenna thought. Then suddenly he was cast as a New York detective in a weekly television drama.

"I want to have your baby," she told him. Getting their girlfriends pregnant was a fad among celebrity men. "Baby bumps" and "baby daddies" were a sensation in the entertainment news. She imagined herself elegantly gowned and round-bellied at a red carpet event with Brad. "Think of what beautiful children we'll have." He was making a ridiculous amount of money.

She stopped taking the medications that were contraindicated in pregnancy and waited to feel the difference. A month passed and she felt fine. In fact, she felt better than ever. The future welled in her throat and sparkled in her mind.

"I'm so happy!" she told Pryzansky. She couldn't help it. She was pregnant. She pressed her lips together and hugged herself, as if physically holding in the news.

"Tell me," he said with unusual interest.

She grabbed for anything. "I just graduated from Clown College!"

"Clown College. I didn't know such an institution existed."

She stifled a laugh. "Oooh, yes. Clowns don't just appear out of thin air! They have to be educated! I got a job as an apprentice clown. Luckily! Because it's not as if there are a lot of clown jobs out there. I'm a female clown, of course. I wear a blue gingham dress with ruffled knickers, and a floppy hat with a big pink flower on top." She stroked her hair. "And long red braids. Because my hair is red already, I don't have to wear a wig, which is great because wigs are so uncomfortable." She looked at Pryzansky's comb-over. "I'm sure you can imagine. I'm one of those clowns that pop out of a tiny car with a bunch of other clowns. A clown car, you know? We come scurrying out of the car and spread through the audience being silly and blowing horns, the usual clown behavior. We aren't really all stuffed in the car. We come up through a trapdoor in the floor and then out of the car. Did you know that? You probably did."

She sighed and sat back. Her lower abdomen felt heavy and she was suddenly tired. She wasn't sure she had the energy to think up much more. "I don't know how you feel about clowns, but there are people who don't like them. There's a certain prejudice against circus and carnival professionals in general: your clowns, your jugglers, your knife throwers; fat ladies, midgets, carnies—carnies especially. Everybody dumps on carnies, even the midgets. If clowns are royalty, carnies are peasants. Actually, the circus hierarchy goes like this: acrobats, lion tamers, *then* the clowns. The other day during a performance I was—"

"This is preposterous," Pryzansky cut in.

"Well, I'm sorry you feel that way," Jenna said. "If you can't tell your psychopharmacologist you're a clown, who can you tell?"

"You are not a clown," Pryzansky said. He looked at the clock on his desk. Their time was almost up. "I don't know what moves you to tell these lies. Psychoanalysis is not my specialty. Here is the name of a doctor I want to refer you to. I'm afraid I can't treat you anymore."

"You're firing me? Who will prescribe my medications?"

"It appears that your medications need some adjustment. But unless you are honest with me, I can't help you, and I don't think, in any case, that medication is the only therapy you need. Dr. Radley is an excellent psychiatrist." He tore the page off his memo pad and handed it to her. "He will prescribe your medications from now on. I beg you to call him immediately."

"But I've never felt better in my life!" Jenna said.

"That's what worries me," Pryzansky said.

Jenna sat on her couch and stroked her stomach, where sturdy little Brad Junior lived like a troll. Pryzansky had to have known she was kidding around. Anyone else would have laughed. And yet a finger of chagrin tap-tapped at her mind like a woodpecker at a tree. Clown College? She had no idea where that came from. She didn't mean him to actually believe her. Obviously! Or she did mean him to, and then she didn't. She couldn't remember what she meant, but she knew for certain that she'd been misunderstood, and felt injured, irate: people were so goddamn stupid. She heard her voice like an echo—*Clowns don't just appear out of thin air!*—and understood it had been too loud. "Use your indoor voice," her mother used to admonish. Pryzansky's office was the size of a closet: a whisper came out like a shout.

"Good day," she said as a test, addressing a crack in the wall. "My name is Jenna. I am seven weeks pregnant." Her voice was modulated and she spoke the truth. "Myron Pryzansky is a prig."

She got up and went to the bathroom and kneeled in front of the toilet. A tide of vomit roared out of her mouth until she was gagging up strings of bile. Her ob-gyn had told her that feeling sick meant the baby was healthy. She thought about phoning Pryzansky. She would tell him she was pregnant and didn't need him: he was contraindicated. She went into the kitchen and ate a bagel and washed it down with a Coke, then went back to the bathroom and vomited again for the pleasure of knowing Brad Junior was growing.

"I *love* being pregnant!" she told her mother on the phone. "Didn't you just love it?" She heard her mother sniff at the other end of the line. She was the kind of woman who kept tissues tucked in her sleeve. Jenna heard a long, honking blow. *Come on,* she thought impatiently. Everyone was so slow! That morning, she had to tell the kid who bagged her groceries to get the lead out and make it snappy.

"Well, not really, darling. I felt awfully sick in the beginning, and then later I—"

"I *love* feeling sick!" Jenna said. "It's this constant, amazing reminder that there is life inside me!"

"That it is," her mother said dryly.

"I can't wait to get really huge." She would be one of those women who let their big bellies show beneath tight T-shirts and slinky dresses. She would be sexy as hell. "There is nothing sexier than a pregnant woman."

Her mother laughed.

"I'm serious! Why is it that when I am being serious, people think I'm funny, but when I'm being funny, people think I'm serious? It's fucking annoying."

"Jenna! Is something the matter?"

"Yes. People are fucking idiotic is what the matter is."

"I wish you wouldn't use that word."

"What, *idiotic?*" There was a silence on the line. "Nobody gets a joke anymore."

"You're in a bad humor," her mother said.

"I am in an excellent humor, Mother." She rarely called her mother *Mother*. She called her *Mom*, like most people. What would Brad Junior call her? *Mommy, Mom, Mother, Mummy?*

"You might have a girl," her mother said.

"What are you talking about?"

"You just called the baby *Brad Junior*. You were saying you wondered what he would call you."

"I was not," Jenna said. "I was thinking about it. I didn't say anything."

"You certainly did, Jenna. I'm not a mind reader."

"Remember how you used to tell me you had eyes in the back of your head?" She laughed and squeezed her aching breasts. She loved the idea of having eyes in the back of her head. Or just one eye, like Cyclops. She walked into the small, empty room that was to be Brad Junior's nursery. Shimmering light streamed between the slats in the blinds, spangled with motes, striping the floor and wall. The light was so beautiful she wanted to photograph it. Aiming her phone, she took pictures from several angles while her mother's voice bleated, "Hello? Hello?"

Brad was cast in a movie in which he played a man who was charged with a brutal murder that was actually perpetrated by his late brother's spirit. *Sins of My Brother*, it was called. A silly idea for a movie, Jenna thought. They moved to Los Angeles, and he worked night and day. When he came home, he was so beat he could hardly pay attention to her. But she liked the house they rented in the hills above Silver Lake. The lake itself was a disappointing reservoir surrounded by chain-link fences, but she could see the snow-capped San Gabriel Mountains through the back windows of the house, and the downtown skyline from the front porch. She had stopped being sick and was showing now, but there was nobody to see her belly unless she got into the car and drove through the traffic to the mall, or visited Brad at work.

"Can't you find something to do?" he asked. "Why don't you take a class again? Audition for something."

"I don't want to audition. I'm pregnant."

"You have four months to go. You can't come to the set every day."

What she wanted to do was to sit in a fat, flowered chair all day long and gaze at the snow-capped mountains. Eventually she succumbed to the urge. It was winter, bright and chilly. The sky above the mountains was an empty wall immune to passing clouds; the valley below was a flat gray grid that stretched for hours and hours. One morning she woke up and the mountains were brown. The snow on the peaks was gone.

"The snow disappeared!" she told Brad when he finally came home. "Yesterday it was there and today it's gone." Did she mean yesterday? Yes, she did, because today was the first day the snow hadn't been there. Or maybe today was the day after the first day. Between Brad's erratic schedule and her habit of dozing off in her chair, it was hard to cut the days apart. She imagined each day as a slice of bread falling away from a loaf.

"What snow?" Brad said.

"On the mountains."

"I don't know what you're talking about."

"Yes, yes, you do! The snow on the mountains out back!"

"Listen. I've been working for eighteen hours. I need some sleep." His hair was sticky with gel, and there was a trace of tan makeup along his jaw. The wrinkles at the corners of his eyes looked like claws, she thought. He was getting old, and so was she, closer to death every day.

"I love you," she said. "God, I love you so much."

"You too, babe." He flopped onto their bed and was immediately asleep.

She went out to the front porch and looked at the skyline. The eucalyptus trees rattled in the breeze. The owner of the house had planted poinsettias by the front steps, but instead of the thick red domes she thought of as Christmas, these were tall and thin and nearly leafless, struggling transplants from holiday pots. By Christmas, Brad Junior would be six months old and she wouldn't be pregnant anymore. She wished there was a way to keep him in her womb forever. That he might be a girl was an unwelcome idea that passed through her mind too often.

"Don't tell me the sex," she'd said to the ultrasound technician, turning her face away from the monitor in case she could see it herself.

"Relax," the technician said. "I'm not allowed to tell you anyway. That's the doctor's job."

"Don't let her tell me!" Jenna said in alarm. What if the doctor blurted it out? You couldn't un-hear something once it was spoken.

"I won't," the technician said. "But it's not the worst thing in the world to know the sex of your baby."

"It *is* the worst thing! Don't force me to hear something I don't want to know."

The technician wiped the lubricant off her belly and turned off the monitor. Jenna got off the table to get dressed. "What a nut," she heard from inside her blouse as the technician left the room.

Remembering this, she asked, "Do you think I'm a nut?" when Brad woke up from his nap.

He frowned at her. "Of course not. Is there anything to eat around here?"

She made him a peanut butter sandwich and a bowl of chicken noodle soup, a combination she had served at the restaurant hundreds of times. She wished she were there now, joking with customers, balancing her tray on her shoulder. She was the best waitress who'd ever worked there. It had been a perfect life.

"Remember?" she said to Brad. "Remember how it used to be?"

She sat down at the table and began to cry. Brad had come to ignore her when she was like this, because she could never say what was wrong.

He stopped eating and looked at her for a moment. "Hey, babe, stupid question. Are you taking your medications?"

Jenna laughed at him, incredulous. "Of course I'm not! I'm pregnant! That would be crazy."

"What?" His eyes widened. His face went slack and pale.

"Oh, Brad," she said sadly. "You're melting."

It was like being in the hospital, except her mother was the nurse, and she slept in her childhood room instead of a ward. A village of pill bottles sat on her night table, each printed with instructions: once a day in the morning, twice a day with meals, two at night before bed, three a day as needed. Her mother dispensed them. Brad was still in Los Angeles playing the murderous spirit's brother.

She lay in the narrow bed and watched her belly grow so large it seemed the baby would weigh a hundred pounds. The view from her window was of rooftops, cylindrical water towers wearing conical hats, and a taller building farther away whose glass facade was gilded at precisely 3:12 every day. On fine days her face was turned to the window, and time passed according to the movement of the sunlight and the shadows. On overcast days her face was turned to the door where her mother checked on her every hour or so. She got up on the days she saw Dr. Radley.

"How is your mood?" was always the first thing he said. Unlike Pryzansky, he had all his hair, and paid close attention to what she said. She had to be careful not to concern him, or her mother, or Brad daily on the phone. They were waiting for her to retrieve herself. She wasn't allowed to be alone.

"Have you been taking pleasure in any activities?"

"I did the crossword puzzle yesterday. I played with my mother's dog."

But he was sharp, nobody's fool. "Your mother doesn't have a dog."

"No."

"Jenna. Why won't you be honest with me?"

He didn't plead, as her mother did. He didn't feel sorry for her. He sat straight in his chair and wore a suit and tie. She was an exasperating patient, she knew. "You have a disease," he had explained the first time she saw him. "Think of yourself as diabetic. Would you neglect to take your insulin?"

What could she say to that? She wasn't diabetic; she had no idea what she would do. "I don't want this baby," she said. "I don't want him in me." As she said it, she felt an elbow, a foot, maybe a head, knock briefly against her bladder.

"What do you mean when you say you don't want your baby, Jenna? Are you trying to shock me the way you tried to shock Dr. Pryzansky?"

"No. Pryzansky is a fool. I wasn't trying to shock him. I assumed he wasn't listening."

"Why is that? Do you feel unheard? Do you think I'm listening to you now?"

"I don't care if you're listening or not."

"That's because you're depressed, Jenna. I am listening. You'll realize that when the medications do their job."

"When will that be again?"

"Four to six weeks. You should be feeling better very soon."

"That will make everyone happy."

"Most importantly, you."

"Yes."

"Isn't that what you want? To feel better?"

"I want to kill myself, I told you that."

Radley sighed. "That's your illness talking. You know that, don't you, Jenna?"

Jenna nodded. She did know, and there was some relief in that. Brad Junior flipped and rolled like an eel inside her, insistently alive.

STICK SHIFT

I WASN'T OFFERED THE OPTION of being given a car, as some girls were, instead of a big dance with all the works: a dance floor and a tent and an open bar, a band and flowers and catered hors d'oeuvres. A car back in those days cost, what? About $6,000, I guess, for a compact, a Chevette or a Ford Fiesta. But a dance, depending on how big it was, could run upwards of double that. Some thought that girls who opted for a car were selfish because they enjoyed the other girls' dances without reciprocating, but as far as I know nobody said so to their faces. There weren't that many of them, anyway.

But, as I say, I wasn't given a choice, and my parents could well afford a dance. They'd thrown one apiece for my two older sisters, who were long gone—one to California, one to marriage—by the time it was my turn. A *coming-out dance* was what it was called, as it had been since the days, eons ago, when it was meant to be a girl's first introduction to Society, though now it was just an excuse for a lavish party, and no one was invited that I didn't already know.

My brother, who was a senior in college, was full of contempt for me, as if he hadn't thoroughly enjoyed going to coming-out dances when he was my age. Conveniently, he had forgotten this, along with a lot of other facts about himself.

"Coming-out! What a farce!" *Farce* was his new word. "I'm surprised at you, Maddy," he said.

I was surprised to hear that he was surprised, that he thought about me at all. He knew I didn't have any say. I was doing as I was told.

"What's it to you?"

"I thought you were different, that's all."

Now I was interested. "Different how?" But he sank back into himself and refused to say, which I took to mean that he didn't know. He was just acting superior, as he often did, for lack of anything better to do than make other people feel inferior.

"Jerk," I said.

"Cretin."

"Stop it," my mother snapped from the living room. When she told you to stop doing something, you stopped. She was in there with the woman who was in charge of the flowers. They were discussing the bouquet I would hold while standing in the reception line at the party. I drifted in and sat on the arm of the couch. The dance was in two days.

"Isn't Madeleine a pretty girl," the woman said.

"*Thank* you," my mother said.

"Thank you," I echoed obediently.

I had no idea about myself, whether I was pretty or different or what. That I had not yet attracted a boyfriend was a failure that weighed on my mind. If I was pretty, I figured, I would have one already. But if I was different, a fresh idea for me, that would explain the problem, for I thought that boys didn't like girls who weren't the same as every other girl they knew. I didn't play varsity sports and look like it, and I wasn't fey. I didn't play an instrument or go in for the arts. I was smart, though. "Boys are intimidated by your intellect," my married sister once told me, meaning it as a compliment. But I didn't act nearly as smart as I was, so I couldn't believe that was true.

"Peonies and foxglove," my mother said to the flower woman, even though arrangements had all been planned out weeks before. She ticked off each item from a list on her lap. "Viburnum around the tent poles. White roses and lady's mantle for the table arrangements. The tablecloths will be teal."

"What color is your gown?" the woman asked me.

"Pink," I said. "It's got a white sash, and a big bow here." I pointed to the right side of my waist.

"It was her sister's," my mother said, which was true, but it had been altered and updated, the sash and bow added on. My mother said that there was no point in wasting an expensive dress that had been purchased in New York City, regardless of how long ago. My friends had dresses they chose for themselves at local boutiques, dresses that I envied despite my belief in the superiority of anything that came from New York.

I noticed the flower woman and my mother had the same hairdo, their hair combed straight back from their foreheads and falling to their shoulders. My mother lit a cigarette and blew the smoke above our heads. I smoked, too, but she didn't know it. She smelled too much like a cigarette herself to smell it on me. She might not have minded, I honestly didn't know, but it was my policy to keep the truth from her until I had some idea how she would receive it.

My best friend Wendy was one of the girls who chose to be given a car. She picked me up after supper, and we drove with all the windows down, smoking cigarettes and singing along with the radio, what girls everywhere do in the summer, until we reached a roadhouse so far out in the country that no one cared how old we were. Sitting at the bar, we ordered rum and cokes and continued our silly conversation. Wendy was not surprised that I was coming out, but perhaps because she had decided against it, we never talked about my dance. We talked about the boys we knew, and the uncharted terrain of sex and college; we talked about our friends and families.

Wendy's mother made heart-shaped waffles and hemmed up the skirts of our school uniforms; she bought Wendy the kind of clothes I wanted and didn't have. But Wendy wasn't smart and would be going to junior college. So we were even in my mind because of that, and because she'd never had a boyfriend either, though I think she thought she was superior because I didn't have anything fashionable to wear when we went out at night. Usually I wore a cotton print skirt and a polo shirt I thought might be sexy because it strained across my breasts. Wendy wore a pair of tight leather pants and a cream silk blouse. I had never told her what my mother once said, that Wendy's family was déclassé.

A couple of guys came in after we had been there a while. They were dressed as if they'd just come from construction jobs, paint and plaster slapped on their jeans. I liked the look of them, and poked Wendy so she'd take notice.

"Gross," she said immediately.

"No, no. Look at the guy in the blue T-shirt." Both of them were much older than us, and the one wearing the blue T-shirt really was nothing special, with acne-scarred skin and thin light brown hair, big muscles popping out from his sleeves. He saw me looking at him and came over. His name was Lance and he said he was a mason.

"My grandfather was a Mason," Wendy said. "It's a secret society, right?"

"Not that kind of mason," Lance said. He didn't elaborate. He sat down on the stool next to me and pointed to my rum and coke. "I bet you're not old enough to drink that."

I could feel the heat climb up my face. I sensed Wendy's impatience on my opposite side. Lance's friend came over and started talking to her, which I knew she would blame me for later.

After telling me that he lived not far from the bar, Lance asked me where I came from as if I'd landed there from somewhere exotic.

"I live in town. Near the museum."

"Swanky," he said.

"It's boring, really." I actually never thought my neighborhood was boring; I never thought about it at all. But now I saw it, as if from above, as a mundane province of houses and lawns.

"That's why you came all the way out here, huh?"

"Yeah, I guess. I'm going to college up north in the fall." I said that to impress him as much as I was impressed with myself, but he drew back and looked at me with an amused expression.

"Slumming, are you?"

I didn't know what that meant.

He shook his head. "Never mind. How about a game of darts?"

I wasn't as bad at the game as I thought I would be, perhaps because of the relaxing effect of the rum I drank faster than I normally would. But I wasn't much of a drinker, so I refused a second round.

"Cheap date," Lance remarked as he paid for a fresh beer. I didn't know what that meant either. I wondered if I should object to being called cheap, but he didn't appear to mean anything by it.

I watched him fling another dart. His friend was talking intently to Wendy while she smoked and looked the other way. *Let's go*, she mouthed at me, but I ignored her and played my turn. Finally she got up and walked toward the ladies room, signaling me to join her there.

"What kind of a name is Lance," was the first thing she said. "He's not even good-looking."

"I think he is. Well, okay, no. But there is something about him."

"Trust me, Maddy, there is nothing about him. How old are they, anyway, thirty? Let's go before they start thinking we like them."

We were talking through the wall of adjacent stalls while we sat on the toilets and peed. The door in front of me was painted a very dark brown, maybe to cover all the old graffiti carved into the wood. WASH YOUR THANG, I read, and MUNGO IS A COCKSUCKER. The room smelled of urine and soap and pot. Someone must have smoked a joint right before we came in. I stood and flushed the toilet, walked out of the stall, and confronted myself in the mirror over the sink. My hair hung past my shoulders, dark and straight. Wendy came out of her stall and said, "You should really go to my salon. Your hair is so..." She looked in the mirror and fluffed her short blond cut.

"So... what?" I was having my hair done for my dance and I didn't know what the hairdresser would do with it. I didn't have any say in that either, and hoped I wouldn't look foolish.

"Boring," she said flatly. "Come on, let's go."

I felt as if I could stay in that reeking bathroom forever, hanging onto one thing without letting go of another.

"You go," I said. "I'm staying. I like Lance, he's nice."

Wendy stared at me. "You're joking."

"No. Honestly. Go."

"God, you really are desperate," she said as she pulled open the bathroom door.

I wondered if Wendy and I would be enemies now, or if the argument would blow over. When I came out of the bathroom, Lance was alone at the bar.

"Where'd your friend go?" I said.

"Your friend wasn't interested, so he left. He only meant to stay for a little while anyway."

"I'm sorry about that. She's kind of a snob."

He nodded and said, "I guess you need a ride home."

He drove a red truck with a white top over the bed and a stick shift on the floor of the cab.

"I've never ridden in a truck," I said with surprise because it seemed to me that I should have.

"You want to drive?" Lance said. "You're more sober than I am."

"I don't know how to use a stick shift."

"Come on, I'll teach you," he said. "Everybody should know how to drive stick."

There was a field next to the bar that we practiced in. It took me a long time to get the motion of stepping on the gas while letting out the clutch, and I stalled so often it got embarrassing.

"Like this," Lance said, moving one hand slowly down as he moved the other up, like a duck's feet in water. When I finally was able to drive forward without stalling, he put his big hand on mine on the stick shift and showed me how to use it.

"You can hear it in the engine," he said. "The sound tells you when to shift up."

I could hear it, and it was satisfying to do the right thing at the right time. But then I made the mistake of shifting into first when I should have shifted to third, causing the truck to stop with such a jolt that we both hit our heads on the ceiling. That scared me so much I wanted to give up, but Lance wouldn't let me.

"You'll be scared forever if you give up now," he said.

"I don't mind," I said, ready to switch places with him.

"Yes, you do, or you wouldn't be here right now."

"Here in a truck, or here with you?" I said.

"Both. You're bolder than you think."

Eventually I was able to drive out onto the road, but I was afraid to go above third gear. We putted along the winding country lanes, which were dark but for the dim lights of a farmhouse every now and then. I sat very close to the steering wheel and stared out the windshield in mute attention. The night air coming through the windows cooled my face. I smelled hay and manure, and the sharp scent of soft tar, for the day had been brutally hot. We passed a pond with a little dock that made me want to go swimming.

"You're doing great," Lance said. But then we came to a crossroads and I did or didn't do something that made the engine sputter out.

"Darn," I said. "I am not good at this."

"Well, I wouldn't want to take you into traffic," Lance said.

"You know what I want to do? I want to go swimming in that pond back there."

Lance turned and looked back at the pond. "What, you've got a bathing suit in that little purse?"

I sat for a moment, trying to figure out what I wanted, or, rather, who I wanted to be. The night was moonless and there were no streetlights on the road.

"I mean skinny-dip," I said.

"Huh. So, you're afraid to drive stick, but *not* afraid to swim naked with a stranger."

"It's not a matter of which I'm more afraid of, it's which I'd rather do. I'm afraid of pretty much everything I've never done, and I haven't done a lot."

"I believe that," he said.

We left the car at the crossroads and crossed the rough pasture to the pond. The water looked impermeable as glass, and I thought of the creatures beneath it, turtles and eels and fish. Not only had I never skinny-dipped with a man before, I had never swum in a pond. I stripped off my clothes and dove off the dock before I could think about it. Immediately I was blinded; the water was cold and black. I swam toward what I hoped was the surface and broke through it with a shriek. Lance's face popped up in front of me and I screamed again in surprise. His wet hair was slicked back from his forehead, making his face look flat and wide.

"Chilly, isn't it," he said in a conversational voice, and swam away from me.

I watched his body slice through the water, his muscled arms smoothly wheeling. At the end of the pond he turned and cut back through his wake to me.

"Nice, once you get used to it," he said. "Your teeth are chattering. Come on, you have to move."

His body was gray beneath the scrim of water. I looked down at mine and saw it was the same. I stopped swimming once I reached the center of the pond.

"We're ghosts," I said. I looked up at the starless sky. Rain had been forecasted for the day of my party.

Lance swam back to me. His irises were black dots against the glowing whites of his eyes. "What are we doing here?"

I knew what he meant. "Swimming."

"Is that all?"

"Maybe."

He hooked one arm around my waist and kissed me on the lips very gently. It was the nicest kiss I'd ever been given, and when he stopped I told him so.

"How many kisses have you had?" he said with a laugh.

"Not many, believe me."

"A beauty like you?"

"I'm not beautiful."

"You are, though," he said. "And even more so for not knowing it."

He kissed me again and it was just as sweet. I felt his hard chest against my breasts. "What do you want?" he said.

"I don't know. What do you think?"

"I'm glad it was me you picked up at that bar, is what I think."

"I didn't pick you up!"

"You surely did. And I'm glad it was me, or you would be in trouble by now. Maybe you were looking for trouble, or thought you were, but you don't know what trouble is."

"What is trouble, then?" I said. Coyly, I admit.

"Not me," he said and let go of my waist. He swam back to the dock.

I went after him and climbed up. My clothes lay in a heap on the boards. My wet hair dripped heavy down my back. Lance had already put on his jeans and was drying his chest with his tee shirt. I got dressed and we walked back to the car. I couldn't see the ground beneath me, the tussocks and divots and rocks. When I stumbled, he said, "Hold my hand," and we walked across the field like that.

"I don't know about anything," I said as we neared the truck. "I've never been in trouble or even close to it. Being with you and skinny-dipping tonight is the wildest thing I've ever done."

He pulled me to him and really kissed me this time, cradling my neck with one hand. There wasn't anything sweet about it, and it left me wanting more.

"You'll do wilder things," he said when he let me go. He made me get into the driver's seat. "Well, go on, then," he said, and I turned the ignition key.

By the time we got to my house, I swung into the driveway as if I'd been driving stick all my life. Lance pulled up the emergency brake for me. He sat back and looked at the house.

"What a monster. I would have hated to lay all that brick. What's going on there in back?"

"Oh, that's a tent. My parents are giving me a party tomorrow night and it's going to be held under there."

"A party under a tent. I never heard of that."

"When I get a car, I'm going to make sure it's a stick shift," I said.

"Is that so?" He chuckled. "You are really something."

"I'm something, all right." I looked up at the house. All the windows were dark. "I just don't know what that something is."

He turned in his seat and looked at me. In the yellow light from the street lamp his face looked ravaged by small scars and pocks.

"You're a striking girl, and you'll know it soon. Beauty is a power as valuable as intelligence, and you'll find that out too. I imagine you won't come back here once you go off to college. I hope you don't. I'd like to meet you again ten years from now, though. I bet you'll be formidable."

"Formidable. There's a word from the SATs."

"I went to college," he said. "I didn't finish, but I went."

"Do you want to come to my party? You have to wear a tuxedo, though. I know guys hate doing that."

"No, I don't want to come to your party. Thanks anyway."

"The beer will be free."

He laughed at that.

The hairdresser put a headful of curlers in my hair, but when she took them out, my hair fell down as lank as ever. She wet my hair again, put the curlers back in and made me sit under a hair dryer for an hour. But my hair refused to curl no matter what. Unable to think of anything else to do, she wound it into a twist at the nape of my neck. Suddenly my New York dress looked dowdy, even my mother had to admit it. Reluctantly, she took me to a shop where I picked out a long sheath that exposed my arms and back. I wouldn't look foolish after all.

Maybe because I liked my hairstyle and dress, I enjoyed myself at my party more than I thought I would. Wendy was friendly again.

"Did you have sex with him?" she asked.

"Yes," I said impulsively. Of course she didn't believe me.

By ten o'clock everybody who was invited had arrived, and the dance floor was packed to its edges. My uncle was pushing me around in a jerking foxtrot when I saw Lance standing a few yards out from the tent, barely visible in the dark. He was wearing a pale blue tuxedo and matching bow tie; white ruffles foamed from his chest. As my uncle led me around and around, I watched him search the crowd. His gaze passed over me once, twice, three times, four. But he didn't find me, and then he was gone.

THE OTHER RACHEL HERSCH

TUESDAY WAS RACHEL'S DAY for the shrink; she went first thing in the morning. "I'm fine," she'd say at the beginning of each session, then go on to complain about her life. She disliked her job at a literary agency, where her task was to read manuscripts and boil their contents down to a single descriptive paragraph. Rarely did she read anything that interested her boss, so her job was to write a formulaic rejection letter to the author and sign with her boss's name.

"My job is to disappoint people," she said.

"You say you don't enjoy your job, but you're not looking for another one," her shrink said. "If you want something to change, you have to change it yourself."

Yet any job she found would be dull and poorly paid: she was twenty-two years old and lucky to have a job at all. It disturbed her that she was bored with her life just as it was beginning. "I thought it would be different," she said.

"How so?" he said. But she couldn't tell him exactly, only that nothing ever happened to her.

"I get up and go to the office. I do my job for eight hours, then I go home."

"What do you do on the weekends?"

"Sleep," she said. "Watch movies."

"Do you go out with friends?"

"Sure," she lied. The only people she knew in the city were her co-workers, the super in her building, and the proprietor of the corner bodega.

"Imagine what it would be like not to have a job."

"I didn't say I don't want a job. I said I thought my life would be different."

She went to the shrink at her parents' insistence because she'd been severely OCD until her senior year in college, when one dripping morning in late February she woke up not caring about shutting the door to her room exactly twelve times, and whether the meat touched the salad on her plate. As if the universe snapped its fingers and brought her out of a trance, and there she was, a normal human being. The transition had been a non-event; she simply forgot to obsess. Her doctor at the time said that sometimes a patient abruptly recovered, or could just as suddenly relapse, without any clinical explanation.

Her parents were afraid she might suffer a setback under the pressures of adult life, though the pressures of adulthood were nothing compared to high school and college, when her condition made her a pariah. She'd organized her schoolwork in color-coded folders, had to have her toothbrush, bristles up, in the precise center of the left hand edge of the sink, insisted her clothes hang an inch apart in the closet; everything she did and how she did it had been a battle in the war against chaos. Now, when she got undressed at night, she dropped her clothes on the floor, then picked through the pile in the morning to find something to wear to work. Her cubicle at the agency was a welter of papers and deli cups, coils of orange peel, candy wrappers, half-empty Diet Coke cans. After years of vigilant orderliness, she'd become a slob.

"So, you're swinging the other direction," her shrink had said. "I think it's natural to want to experiment with a different way of living. You'll sort it out in time."

He hadn't known her in her OCD days. No one who knew her now did. For a time, she'd considered changing her name; that was how different she felt. Instead, she got a tattoo of a phoenix on her shoulder, to symbolize rebirth, a thing her former self wouldn't have done in a million years out of fear of germs and infection.

After her appointment, she went to work. Her boss, Phillip, was a Buddhist; he closed his door to meditate every afternoon, and emerged fifteen minutes later looking beatific and smug. He called her *Raquel* when he was in a good mood, which she thought he should always be in: what was all that meditating for if not to provide him with inner peace?

"Nice session?" he asked because he knew it was her day for the shrink. She'd wanted permission to come in a little late on Tuesdays, and couldn't in the moment think of another excuse. He went to a shrink, too, on Friday afternoons, which she knew because she answered his phone and kept his schedule, and was the one to call if he couldn't make the appointment. "What did you talk about?" he teased. He was utterly unprofessional.

"You," she said without looking up from a rejection she was writing for a book by a woman who raised a hippopotamus from birth. The story had been intriguing until it became clear that the hippopotamus was never going to attack anyone.

Dear Ms. Kellerman, Thank you for the opportunity to read Hippo Days and Hippo Nights. Interesting though it is, it's not quite right...

"Do you know a guy named Neal Price?" Phillip asked.

"Nope."

"Because he went to your college. He graduated a year ahead of you."

She stopped typing. "Neal Price," she said, pretending to think.

"He said he knows you, or knows of you. He said they called you Rigid Rachel. I said, 'No way!'" Daintily, with his thumb and forefinger, he tweezed a Snickers wrapper from her desk. "'That is definitely not the Raquel I know.'"

She looked up at him and forced a laugh. "Rigid Rachel! No, he's thinking of the *other* Rachel Hersch. It was such a pain having the same name. I used to get her junk mail all the time."

"I knew it," Phillip said.

"Yeah."

He leaned on the wall of her cubicle. "So, what was the deal with the other Rachel Hersch?"

Rachel shrugged. She wondered how her name had come up. Phillip had obviously mentioned her, but why? "How well did your friend say he knew her?"

"Not my friend yet! But I'm hoping. We have a date tonight." Phillip was thirty and looking for a steady boyfriend. He wanted to settle down. "Fingers crossed. He's as cute as a button. And a vegetarian!"

"Fingers crossed." She held up her crossed fingers until he was out of sight, then immediately searched Facebook for Neal Price's page. He was pictured standing on a white sand beach in the fruit punch glow of a sunset. He had 2,422 friends. She didn't recognize him at all.

When she got off work that evening, the first thing she did was go to a hair salon down the street from her apartment building. She'd torn an advertisement out of the newspaper to show the stylist what she wanted.

"Well, but that girl is blond," the stylist said.

"I know," Rachel said. "I want to be blond and have a hairstyle like that." The model's hair was cut severely short, exposing her neck and ears, with longer bangs swept across her brow. Rachel's straight, puddle-colored hair bluntly grazed her shoulders in a style she'd worn all her life.

"Okay," the stylist said. "But if you change your hair this drastically, you're going to have to reconsider your whole look. You need to wear makeup with a haircut like this, eyeliner and mascara at least."

"Got it. What else?"

The stylist appraised her. "You're thin enough, but your clothes are kind of lame. Get yourself a couple of tight tops and skinny jeans. A black pencil skirt, you got one of those?"

Rachel shook her head. "But I'll get one."

The stylist looked at the picture again. "A makeover, huh? What, are you on the lam?"

Rachel smiled. "Kind of."

As she watched the majority of her hair fall to the floor, she felt exhilarated and frightened at once. She'd chosen the new hairstyle because it was as different as possible from her own without considering if it would suit her. Perhaps she should have given it more thought, yet it thrilled her to do something so rash. She read *People* and *Us* as the stylist glopped dye on her hair, and then went on to *Glamour* as she waited for the color to take, examining how celebrities made up their faces and admiring the latest clothes. She never cared about any of that before—what a nerd she had been! *Rigid Rachel.* She'd been unaware that people called her that. Living so much in her tormented mind, that she was conspicuous had never occurred to her.

Once the dye was rinsed out of her hair, the stylist sat her in front of the mirror and pulled the towel away. "It's not too late," she said. "I can dye it brown again."

Rachel stood up and looked closely at her reflection. Her hair was so blond it was nearly white. Tentatively, she touched it, as if it were someone else's. She ran her fingers through it.

"What do you think?" the stylist said doubtfully.

"I love it," Rachel said.

She called in sick for the next two days. First she went to an optometrist, then shopping. She bought the sort of clothes the stylist suggested, and a bag of makeup to experiment with. For the first time in years, she longed for the companionship of another girl. She'd had friends when she was a kid, before the OCD set in; she remembered the freedom, specific to childhood, of thinking about nothing much. When she was satisfied that she'd done as good a job as she was capable of, she returned to the hair salon.

"Well?" she said to the stylist.

The stylist stepped back. "Jesus Christ. You look completely different."

"Would you recognize me at all?" Rachel asked.

"Not if I didn't know."

The receptionist at the agency's front desk asked her whom she'd come to see.

"Phillip Casen," Rachel said.

"I'm afraid you need an appointment to see Mr. Casen," the receptionist said. She stared when Rachel revealed who she was. "What in the world?"

"It was time for a change," Rachel said.

"There are changes and there are changes," the receptionist said. "Has Phillip seen you yet?" She buzzed Rachel in, and Rachel walked down the hall to her cubicle. A few of the other assistants looked up as she passed, but didn't appear to recognize her. She stood at the door of Phillip's office and waited until he noticed.

"May I help you?" he said in a snotty voice. She laughed, and he said, "Raquel? Is that you?"

"It's me," she said. "What do you think?"

"I think—wait, are your eyes green?"

She nodded. "Contacts."

"You look amazing," he said. "But weird. It's as if your voice is coming out of someone else's head." He looked her up and down. "I don't think I've ever seen you wear high heels. Platinum blonde! Interesting choice. You're quite glamorous, really, not the girl I hired at all."

"You're saying I was dowdy before." He didn't disagree. "Well, this is me now," she said.

She went to her desk and reapplied her lipstick using the mirror in her new compact. She could not get enough of looking at herself. She felt inexpressibly beautiful.

Dear Mr. Lennon, Thank you for the opportunity to read A YEAR IN TEN DAYS. Interesting though it is, it's not quite right... She deleted the lines, and began again.

Dear Joshua Lennon, A YEAR IN TEN DAYS is well written, but it falls apart at the end. We never find out why Signe ran away, and Dash's sexuality issues are unresolved. It's as if you got bored and didn't want to think about it anymore, and I can't say I blame you because the characters aren't very interesting. If you're bored writing it, you can be sure that we'll be bored reading it—something to consider when writing your next novel, which you should do because you obviously have talent. Best, Rachel Hersch, Assistant to Phillip Casen. She clicked send, and went on to the next one.

Dear Helen Pool, VERONA is a thinly disguised plagiarism of Edith Wharton's short story "Roman Fever." I didn't get a degree in Comparative Literature for nothing. Sincerely, Rachel Hersch, Assistant to Phillip Casen.

Dear Mayer Borsall, WHAT KIND HEART is a beautifully written book, but my boss doesn't usually represent first novels because they don't make him any money. You'll probably run up against this prejudice again before you find an agent, but do persist! I foresee great things. Best Wishes, Rachel Hersch, Assistant to Phillip Casen

During her lunch hour, she went to a secondhand store and bought some colorful bangles and a long turquoise necklace that swung fetchingly over her breasts. Jewelry used to be just another possession to keep track of, but now she had an urge to be festooned. As she was walking back to the office, she saw Phillip at a table at an outdoor café with a young man who resembled Neal Price's Facebook photo. She crossed to the other side of the street and walked along with her face averted, but realized her striking hair color made her recognizable when she heard Phillip calling her name. She walked on as if she hadn't heard him, and was back at the office long before he returned.

"I saw you on the street!" he said. "I was at the Star Café with Neal."

"Oh yeah?" She gave him a mystified look.

"Neal Price, you know, the cutie who went to your college."

"Right, your friend."

"He's adorbs," Phillip gushed. "You have to meet him."

Her computer pinged. It was an email from Mayer Borsall.

Dear Rachel Hersch, I can't tell you how much I appreciated your email. Your encouragement is flattering, and your candor refreshing. Would you have a drink with me sometime? Writing is a lonely business, and I sense a kindred spirit in you. Sincerely, Mayer Borsall

"Who's that from?" Phillip said, craning his neck to get a view of her screen.

"Nobody. A friend. Why?"

"You looked, I don't know, shocked."

"Indigestion," she said, putting a hand to her mouth. She waited for Phillip to go into his office before turning back to the email. She clicked reply.

Dear Mayer, I would be delighted to meet you for a drink. When? Where? I look forward to hearing. Rachel Hersch

When Mayer hadn't replied by the next day, she told herself to forget about him. Phillip was always saying writers were flaky. She was contemplating her inbox when from behind her a voice said, "Excuse me? I'm looking for Phillip Casen's office?"

She swiveled around. It was Neal Price. He wore khaki pants and a blue linen blazer; one hand jingled the change in his pocket. He looked older than his Facebook picture, his hair darker and shorter. "Down the hall, first left," she said, and swiveled back to her computer.

"Wait, you're Rachel, right?"

Reluctantly, she turned.

"I'm Neal, Phillip's friend. I think you and I went to the same college?"

"Did we?" she said coolly. "Oh, yes. Phillip told me about you. I don't think we've met before."

"What was your major?"

"Comp Lit."

"Economics."

"So our paths wouldn't have crossed."

He frowned. "I must have seen you around because you look familiar."

"People tell me that all the time," she said. "I guess I have one of those faces."

"So, did you know the other Rachel Hersch?"

"Did you?"

"I had a class with her once. She always sat in the same seat. I remember she would rub the top of the desk. She'd sit down and rub her hand around like three or four times. Sometimes she'd stand up and sit down and do it again, like she hadn't gotten it right the first time. Who knows what was going on in her head."

Three revolutions, she thought. Exactly three. She could feel the cool veneer growing warm beneath her palm, the physical need to touch it. Because if she didn't rub the desk three times in a perfectly round, clockwise motion, she would be too agitated to sit through the class. After she rubbed the desk, she'd check her tote bag to see if it held everything she'd put in it before she left her room. She'd check it, then check it again a moment later, then again a moment after that. She could never be sure. Someone might have taken something while her head was turned. All sorts of things could have happened.

"I wonder where she is now," Neal said.

She looked at him. He was so handsome and relaxed. "Did you ever feel sorry for her?"

"Not really, no. I guess I should have, huh?"

Phillip came around the corner. "Neal!" They bussed each other's cheeks. "What are you talking about? Who should you feel sorry for?"

"The other Rachel Hersch," Neal said at the same time as Rachel said, "Nobody you know."

The next morning she left her apartment and got as far as the subway station before she had to go back and check if she'd locked her door. She'd locked it—of course she had! She unlocked it, and then locked it again so she would remember she'd done it this time, then left the building and only got to end of the block before she had a sinking feeling that the door was unlocked. She went back. The door was locked. "The door is locked," she said aloud. Still, she turned back and checked again.

Hearing Neal Price describe the other Rachel Hersch had unraveled her to a single thread. Until now, she had forgotten the consolation her rituals gave her, the panic she felt when denied them, the necessary habits that pulled her through the day as if through the eye of a needle. When she reached the office, she cleared her desk and arranged everything at right angles to one other. She put her purse where she always did, in the bottom left hand desk drawer. She opened the drawer. Still there. She opened and closed the drawer every ten minutes, then took her purse and put it in plain sight, on the shelf above her desk.

"What's with your desk?" Phillip said when he came in.

"I cleaned it," she said.

"But why? Did you see a cockroach or something?"

"No!" she said as if one had suddenly crawled across her keyboard.

"Chill," he said. "Just kidding."

Once the idea was in her mind, she couldn't get it out. That a cockroach might appear out of nowhere made her eyes stray from her computer and scan her desk every couple of minutes. Her phone rang.

"Rachel! It's Neal."

"Hang on, I'll transfer you to Phillip."

"No, I wanted to talk to you."

"Me? Why?" She peered behind her computer. Nothing was back there at the moment.

"A few of us will be hanging out at Bar Fifty-Three later on, I thought you might want to join us."

"A few of who?"

"Friends from school. We hang out about once a month, so we won't lose touch." He went on to name a couple of girls Rachel had never heard of. "Phillip said you haven't lived in the city that long. Maybe you want to meet some new people."

"He said that? What else did he say?"

"Just that," he said with a laugh. "Is there something else I should know?"

I am the other Rachel Hersch, she imagined telling him, and for a second she thought she had. "Okay," she said. "It sounds like fun."

After she hung up, she took her compact from her purse and looked in the little round mirror. She looked exactly the same as the last time she'd checked, but she was nevertheless surprised not to be confronted by her old self. She put the compact away and straightened her desk again. Her computer pinged. It was Mayer.

Dear Rachel, Excuse me for not responding to your email sooner. I'll be honest and admit that I extended my invitation in an uncharacteristically bold, possibly insane, moment, and then immediately regretted it. The prospect of meeting a woman for drinks and conversation fills me with dread. I say "woman," but really mean "anyone." I am crippled by social anxiety; it's been a problem all my life. I don't expect you to understand, nobody ever does. Sincerely, Mayer Borsall

She stared at the screen for a while, tapping her fingernail on her keyboard. *Dear Mayer, I understand more than you think.*

Bar Fifty-Three was only a few blocks from her office. It was October, and the evening was dim. The bar seemed to be lit only by jack o' lanterns. She heard rather than saw Neal until her eyes adjusted.

"This is who I was telling you about," he said to two girls who sat with him in a booth. "Meet the other Rachel Hersch."

"I didn't know there was another," one of the girls said. Her hair was almost as blond as Rachel's. "Neal said you majored in Comp Lit. So did I, but I don't remember you. What dorm were you in?"

"Willis Hall," Rachel said as she sat down next to Neal. She recognized the girl from some of her classes.

"I lived in Willis," the other girl said. Her brown hair was short and she wore glittery cat eye glasses. She studied Rachel in the flickering candlelight. "You look familiar."

"I can't stay," Rachel said. Looking around at their unblinking eyes, the atmosphere more shadow than light, she felt as if she were telling them a ghost story, ludicrous yet frightening. A fine layer of perspiration sprang from her pores; in a minute she would be sweating. She could not imagine why she had thought this would be all right. Pretending she wasn't the other Rachel Hersch felt even more uncomfortable than being her. "You were so nice to invite me, but my parents came into town unexpectedly and I have to go meet them now." She thought it sounded like a plausible excuse. People's parents did show up.

Neal made a sad face, and said, "What, all the way from Michigan?"

"Well, I forgot they were coming. I mean, I knew they were, I just got the date wrong. Anyway, they're here now and they have tickets for the theater."

"Cool," he said. "Have fun."

"You know what?" the girl with the glasses said. "You actually look like Rachel Hersch."

"Well, I am Rachel Hersch."

"The other Rachel Hersch, I mean."

"No, she doesn't," the blond girl said. She smiled at Rachel, clearly the nicer of the two. "The other Rachel Hersch was in a few of my classes. You don't look like her at all. She was super frumpy."

"So I've heard," Rachel said as she stood up. She made herself walk at a normal pace until she was outside on the street, then she ran away as fast as she could, her high heels clacking on the pavement in a soothing rhythm until she didn't have the breath to go on.

"We can try an antidepressant," her shrink said. "But that will take a while to kick in. In the meantime, I'll prescribe something for your anxiety. That should help dull the repetitive thoughts."

"And every other thought, too," Rachel said.

He looked at her with pity. "There is always cognitive therapy."

"What am I going to do?" she said. "My life doesn't have room for this. I can barely do my job between searching for insects and organizing my emails. I'm going to get fired, and then what will happen to me?" Her shrink's diplomas and certificates hung on the wall across the room as if he'd put them up over a period of years with no organizational plan. She snapped a red rubber band on her wrist, putting a temporary halt to the thoughts that rushed through her mind like a pack of yapping dogs. "They called me Rigid Rachel," she said. "They watched me."

"Did you think you were invisible?" said her shrink.

She shook her head. It wouldn't take long for Neal and his friends to figure out that there was only one Rachel Hersch; they probably already had. "I didn't think about it at all."

After her appointment, she took the subway to the salon near her apartment.

"Dye it brown," she told the stylist.

"What? Why? I thought you loved it!"

"It's not me."

For the second time, she sat with dye glopped on her hair, waiting for the color to take. She didn't read any magazines. She stared out the window at a patch of half-mowed back garden, the lush and weedy grass at one end abruptly sheared to dry stubble. When the stylist rinsed the dye from her hair, she looked at herself in the mirror.

"You're a pretty girl," the stylist said. "I didn't much care for the blond on you."

"Really? I thought it looked cool."

"Then why didn't you keep it?"

"I told you. It wasn't me." She turned the chair and examined her reflection, inhabiting herself again. Reflexively, she picked up her purse. "This is me," she said as she checked to see that everything was still in its place.

What Brings You Down

Jamison's mother broke her leg at the movie theater by tripping and falling on a flight of stairs that was illuminated by strips of light so people wouldn't trip and fall. Jamison's father wasn't there. It was Jamison's aunt who called from the hospital. She was older than his mother, but steadier on her feet.

"Have you called Catherine?" he asked her. Catherine was his sister.

"No, dear, I thought you would do that."

So Jamison called his sister. At forty-three, Catherine had just given birth to her fifth child. It took her a while to come to the phone.

"Well, it was bound to happen sooner or later," she said. "You've seen how much she's aged."

"I hadn't noticed, to tell you the truth."

"When was the last time you were home?" she said.

"I *am* home," Jamison said, looking around his apartment, which was on the garden floor of a townhouse in Philadelphia. He had been watching *Breaking Bad* on Netflix when his aunt called, and almost hadn't picked up the phone.

"Oh, for God's sake, Jamie. You know what I mean."

"Sometime in the recent past. Christmas?"

"That was eight months ago! Well, you better get down there now, or as soon as you can. You know how useless Daddy is."

"Me? Why not you?"

"I have a three-week-old infant sucking at my breast," Catherine said.

Jamison grimaced. "Thank you for that revolting visual."

"I thought you'd appreciate it. Obviously I can't go anywhere right now. I wish I were like you, free and easy, able to just turn the key in the door."

"If that were true, you wouldn't have birthed that brood of yours."

"Don't be mean," Catherine said. "I was never as smart as you."

Jamison wasn't exactly free and easy, but he was a writer and set his own schedule. He was single and childless. Though he'd had a book published and wrote articles for magazines, his parents, in particular his father, refused to put to rest their belief that he was always on the lookout for a job.

He drove down to Virginia instead of flying. It took half a day to get there. He went straight to the hospital.

"Oh, my sweet boy is here," his mother said in her public voice. "Do I look like a fright?"

"Not at all." Someone had given her lipstick and powder. She looked, he thought, like a corpse who'd been made up to appear alive.

"Where is Daddy?" he said.

"Why, at home! Or, no, I think it's his golf afternoon."

"And Aunt Puddy?"

"Oh, she went back to Baltimore. She was only meant to be here for the weekend."

"She might have stayed." Jamison sat down.

"She had Uncle How to get back to."

"And Daddy could have given up his game."

His mother considered this. "It's easier, frankly, without him. He kept asking the nurses to make him a cup of tea." She wrung her hands. They were so spotted they were nearly brown. "They're letting me go soon. I was hoping you would take me home."

A social worker came by before his mother was discharged. She wanted to know about home care. Jamison looked at his mother, hoping she would have already thought of a plan.

"Well, there's Nella," she said after a moment, referring to the maid. "And Irene."

"Who is Irene?" Jamison said.

"Oh, she does all sorts of things for Daddy and me. We just couldn't live without her."

"What sort of things?" the social worker asked.

"Let's see. She planted a beautiful perennial border out front. And she drives me to the store. And she helps me pay the bills. You know how terrible I am with those."

The social worker and Jamison looked at each other. She handed him a card for a nursing service and said, "I think they can send over someone this evening."

A black woman named Pauline showed up just as Nella was leaving. Physically helping his mother, even tucking her into bed, made something in Jamison's gut shrivel; he could not wait to get out of her room.

"Where are you going?" she said drowsily. She had been given a Valium.

"I'll be right back," he said, and went outside for a walk.

It was August and the cicadas were deafening. Within minutes Jamison's shirt was soaked and sweat dripped from his face to the pavement. How had he withstood this heat growing up? Strangely, he had no memory of it. What he remembered was driving his parents' car at night, his elbow out the open window, repeatedly passing the one gay bar he knew of, underage and ignorant. He remembered spending hours in the pool at the club, watching the older guys horsing around. He hadn't been an effeminate boy; he played second base on his high school team. Luckily, he'd flown under the radar and was considered a regular kid. But he didn't remember a time when he hadn't known he was gay, and had lived with the knowledge for so long that by the time he came out his parents' shock actually shocked him.

He dug his cell phone from his pocket and called his sister.

"How is Daddy?" she asked after he told her about their mother.

"The same." He'd seen his father watching television in the den but what with getting his mother upstairs and briefing the nurse, he hadn't thought to say hello.

"The same as what?"

"God, it's hot here. Was it this hot when we were kids?"

"I don't know how hot it is, Jamie, I'm not there."

He hung up and went back to the house. He wiped his face and neck with some paper towels and went into the den.

"Hi Daddy."

His father looked up from the evening news. "Jamie!" he said with surprise. "Have a seat! Help yourself to a drink. Nuts?" He held up a cut-glass dish of cashews.

"Not as far as I know." Jamison laughed. His father frowned. "Nuts," Jamison said. "It's a joke. Forget it."

"What brings you down?" his father asked.

Rainy days, Jamison thought, shopping malls. "I came down for Mother," he said. "Aunt Puddy called me. About her fall."

"Have you been swimming?" his father said, looking at Jamison's shirt.

"The thing is, she's going to need care until her leg heals. Nurses, probably round-the-clock, at least until we see how she does."

"Nonsense," his father said. "Nella and Irene can take care of her."

"Nella is sixty-four, Daddy. She's not strong enough to help Mother bathe and go up and down the stairs, and somebody has to make the meals. Who is this Irene character?" Why did he call her a character, he wondered? It was the sort of thing his father would say. "What is her job here? How often does she come in?"

"Well, I don't exactly know," his father said. He pushed his eyeglasses up his nose and returned his attention to Brian Williams.

Irene showed up the next afternoon, breezing in through the back door wearing a pair of hip-hugging jeans and a tank top that showcased her deep cleavage. An inch of brown roots grew into her long yellow hair.

"I know who you are!" she said. "You're Jamison, aren't you? I've seen your picture on Violet's nightstand. Her and Harry talk about you all the time. So, what brings you down?"

Possibly you do, Jamison thought. "I'm here because Mother broke her leg over the weekend. I came to..." What indeed had he come to do? Wandering the house all morning, unable to settle down to his work or concentrate on the book he was reading, he'd had a desultory chat with the nurse who took over from Pauline, then went outside and was driven back in by the heat.

"Violet broke her leg? Oh my God! Why didn't anyone call me?" She rushed upstairs to his mother's room, leaving him in the hall. "Violet, sweetie!" he could hear her say. She was a loud talker. He couldn't hear his mother's voice. "How did this happen? Are you in pain? Are these your pills? Let me help you into a fresh nightie. Oh, you've already done that?" She was talking to the nurse now, Jamison guessed. "How many of these is she supposed to have? Are you here for the whole day? That's what I thought. Let me get you a nice cold glass of tea," she said to his mother. "Back in a tick."

She came galloping down the stairs. "Where is poor Harry, in the den?"

"What exactly do you do for my parents?" he said.

"Everything," she said as she whizzed past him. "Harry!" he heard her say. "Has anyone made you lunch?"

He called his sister. "Who is this woman Irene? Have you heard of her before?"

"She used to be their gardener," Catherine said. "Then Mother lost her license after that fender bender and Irene started driving her to the store. Now she helps them do whatever they can't manage. She's become indispensable."

"Have you met her?" Jamison said.

"At Easter. She's something else, isn't she?"

"Mother says she helps her pay the bills."

"Really. I didn't know that." There was a silence between them. "That could be a problem."

"Well, I can't stay here forever," Jamison said.

"You've been there less than twenty-four hours," Catherine said. "Please just make sure Mother is taken care of, okay? Call the nursing service and set up a firm schedule. I'll get down there as soon as I can."

Jamison called the service, packed his bag and kissed his mother goodbye.

"You're leaving me?" she said.

"Cathy will be down soon."

"How soon?"

"Very soon."

It wasn't until he reached the interstate that he realized he'd forgotten to say goodbye to his father.

Jamison visited some straight friends, a married couple, in Nantucket over Labor Day weekend. Another gay man had been invited as well. The other man's name was James, but everyone called him Jamie.

"That's funny," Jamison said. "*Jamie* is what my family calls me; it was my name growing up."

"I didn't know that," his hostess said. "Why didn't you keep it?"

"I wanted to be taken seriously in college. I was a very earnest student. I didn't think *Jamie* suited me. No offense," he said to Jamie.

Jamie laughed. He laughed easily, his teeth white against his summer tan. "None taken. I was an absolute slacker in college. I don't think I grew up until I was about thirty."

They all laughed at that because he was only thirty-five, and for all his supposed slacking off, was a thoracic surgeon now. Jamison liked him more than he'd liked anyone in years. They took a walk on the empty beach after dinner, letting the waves wash over their feet. Just as Jamie leaned in to kiss Jamison, his breath still sweet from dessert, Jamison's cell phone rang.

"Is this Mister Jamison?" a strange voice said. "This is Sherry from Ever Care."

"Ever Care?" Jamison said. "No thank you, whatever it is."

"Ever Care Nursing," Sherry said. "I look after your mother, Miss Violet? I am calling to give you my notice. I know how to do my job, Mister Jamison. I won't be interfered with."

"How are you being interfered with?" Jamison asked. Jamie crossed his arms and looked out to sea.

"And another thing is I think she is the one taking your mother's pills. She is accusing us, but I think it's her and that boyfriend of hers."

"Who? Which pills? What boyfriend?"

"Anyway, I'm leaving now. I guess Geraldine will be here in the morning."

"Now, as in this minute?" Jamison said. But Sherry had already hung up.

While Jamie sat on the sand, Jamison found Ever Care's number and asked for an immediate replacement. Then he called his sister's cell.

"God it's gorgeous out here!" she said.

"Where is out there?"

"Colorado!" she said. "The J-Bar Ranch. I told you. We're here for a week."

"What about the suckling baby?" he asked.

"He's portable," his sister said. "The kids are having a ball."

"Great," said Jamison. He told her about Sherry's call. "I have no idea what she's talking about."

"Well, you better get down there," Catherine said.

"Why not you this time?"

"Are you deaf? I'm in Colorado!"

Jamison left Nantucket in the morning, and was in Virginia by late afternoon.

"What's going on?" he asked his mother, who was sitting up in a wheelchair. She looked tired, and thinner, and paler than before. She wasn't wearing makeup. A feather of worry tickled his mind.

"Absolutely nothing," his mother said. "Occasionally I get a visitor."

"I got a call from a nurse named Sherry who seemed pretty upset."

"Oh, Sherry," his mother scoffed. "She was no good."

"How so?"

"Well, she just wasn't. I don't know. Irene didn't like her. Thank goodness for Irene. She's been doing everything."

"Such as?"

"Making sure Nella and the nurses are paid. Going to the bank for Daddy."

"Are you sure that's a good idea?"

"You have a better one?" his mother said.

He talked to the nurse on duty.

"I don't want any trouble," the nurse said. "But that Miss Irene, she acts like she's the Queen of Sheba. Your mother is such a lady. But Miss Irene gets all up in your face. She accused me of taking a sweater. A sweater in this heat? I found it in your mother's bottom drawer."

"Please don't quit," Jamison said.

"Oh, it takes more than that," she said.

Irene arrived the next morning in Jamison's father's Mercedes. It purred into the driveway. She appeared to be listening to the end of a song on the radio before she got out with a bag of groceries.

"Is that my father's car?" Jamison said.

"Well, I can't be expected to use my own car if I'm running all over town."

"You kept it overnight."

"Uh huh." She handed him the groceries.

"Listen, Irene, I got a call from the nurse who quit the other evening."

Irene sighed. "She isn't the first one I've had to let go."

"But she quit."

"Well, that's her story. You know how they are."

"The nurses?" Jamison said.

"*Blacks*," Irene said, silently mouthing the word.

Jamison didn't know what to say to that. Nothing seemed like the best idea. "What's this about pills? Was she talking about Mother's Valium?"

"I had to refill the bottle twice last week."

"And you think the nurses are stealing them."

"They sell them downtown."

"Really? How do you know that?"

She looked at him as if he were clueless. "Common knowledge, Jamie. That's what they do."

Out of the whole conversation, what bothered him most was that she called him Jamie instead of Jameson.

He went to his father. "Daddy, Mother says Irene goes to the bank for you. Does she have your PIN for the ATM?"

"Of course she does," his father said. "How else is she going to get the cash?"

"I think you should change your PIN and use the ATM yourself."

"Why would I do that?"

"Because we don't know Irene all that well, and you've given her access to your account. She might take money for herself."

"She is only allowed two hundred dollars each time," his father said.

"Well, but...are you there when she takes it out?"

"Now, what would be the point of that? If I were there I could do it myself."

"That's my point, Daddy. I think you should do it yourself."

"Don't have to," he said. "I have Irene."

Later that night, he looked in on his mother. She lay under a light blanket, the bulk of her cast looking like a hidden animal. She seemed to be sleeping deeply, but then she opened her eyes.

"Come and sit next to my bed, darling."

Jamison sat down. "Listen, Mother, I want to talk to you about Irene."

"I know it," she said in a matter-of-fact voice, the voice Jamison thought of as really hers. "She is as trashy as she can be. But she's amusing and she's willing, and we need someone to help us. Who cares if she pockets a few Valium or takes fifty dollars?"

"I do," he said. "I don't like it at all. That kind of dishonesty doesn't have limits. And she bothers the nurses. She's bigoted."

"In a month this cast will come off and I won't need any nurses. I know Irene, I know what she's capable of. She's trash, but she's not a criminal."

"I'm surprised you're letting yourself be taken advantage of, Mother. You're too smart for that."

"I'm not being taken advantage of. I know perfectly well what she's doing."

When Jamison got back to Philadelphia, he briefly reconnected with Jamie, whose hours at the hospital were unpredictable. He got another call from a nurse named Helen who threatened to quit but was persuaded to stay on. It was his sister's turn to go to Virginia.

"I can't," she said. "I have mastitis."

"You're making that up," Jamison said. "I have never, ever heard of it."

"Well, you wouldn't have," Catherine said. "It's an infection of the breast, and it's very painful. Women get it from nursing."

"That is really unfair," Jamison said. "I'm seeing someone now. Or trying to. We have a date tomorrow night."

"What is this, Rock, Paper, Scissors? I'll go down the next time, I swear."

When Jamison got to Virginia he was surprised to be told that his mother was in the hospital. He found her alone in a double room, looking two sizes too small for her bed. Her cast had been removed.

"Grim, aren't they?" she said. "Hospital rooms."

"I'll have some flowers sent over right away," Jamison said. "Why are you here? Nella didn't seem to know."

"The leg is not healing," she said. "They're deciding whether to put a pin in the bone, which may or may not be successful, I'm told.

I don't know." She looked out the window. "This is getting rather tiresome."

Jamison was at a loss. It *was* tiresome. He tried to think of something happy to say.

"I'm seeing someone." He blushed. "Well, we've only gone out a few times, but I have a feeling it could turn into something serious."

His mother turned back to him and smiled. "I'm so glad."

"Yes, well. He's a man."

"I assumed so. You're still gay, aren't you?"

"I thought you were in denial about that."

"I was, it's true. For quite a long while I thought you were mistaken. It's like being told someone you love is leaving you—you hold out hope that they'll change their mind."

"Has someone you love ever left you?" Jamison said.

"Oh, yes. When I was twenty-one I was in love with a musician, a jazz pianist. My parents were scandalized. I would have married him. I would have done anything for him."

"Why did he leave you?"

"He was Jewish. He wanted a Jewish wife."

"You were heartbroken."

"I thought I'd die." Her eyes swam even still at the memory. Jamison pretended to be interested in the ceiling. When he looked at her again, she was composed, her hands clasped in her tiny lap.

"I never knew about that," he said.

"Well, you don't tell your children that their father was your second choice."

"No, I suppose not." He wanted to ask if she loved his father, but realized that she would say yes regardless of how she felt.

The hospital nurse brought in a tray that had a plate of brown meat under gravy and some slimy-looking green beans. He watched his mother eat. Then she laid her head back on the starched white pillow and fell asleep.

When he got back to the house he found a strange man sitting with Irene in the kitchen. He wore plaster-splattered jeans and a sleeveless undershirt that showed off his muscled arms.

"Hello, I'm Jamison," Jamison said, extending his hand.

"Hey," the man said, ignoring Jamison's hand. Not even looking at Jamison, in fact.

Irene smiled brightly and said, "Bobby, this is Violet and Harry's son! Bobby's been helping patch those leaks in the roof. You been over to the hospital to see your mom?"

"What leaks in the roof?" Jamison could see his father in the den watching the television news. "Has my father had dinner yet?" he asked.

"We just called out for a pizza," she said.

"Pizza!" Jamison said.

"Oh yeah, Harry loves pizza," Bobby said.

Jamison went into the den. "Hi, Daddy."

His father looked up. "Jamie! My goodness! What brings you down?"

"Daddy, do you like pizza?"

"Never had it," his father said.

Jamison turned and went back to the kitchen. "Get out," he said.

Irene looked at him as if he were talking to someone else. "Get what out?"

"Yourself. Get out. You and your boyfriend. I don't want to see you here again. Give me the keys to the Mercedes. Now. I mean it." He realized he was trembling. Bobby looked at him with mild interest. Irene's face became an angry mask.

"You can't tell me what to do. You're not the boss of me. Who's going to take care of Violet and Harry? Not you." She sneered. "You don't give enough of a shit about them to come down here more than once a year."

"Actually, I do give a shit about them, and I am here now." He picked up her purse, heavy as a suitcase, and held it out to her. It occurred to him that she probably had something in there that she'd taken from his mother, but whatever it was, she could have it. He would be glad to replace both it and her.

He watched them leave the kitchen, and heard the front door slam. He knew she'd be back tomorrow, or the next day, or the day

143

after that, but he would be there to send her away. After a while, he made his father a ham sandwich and brought it to him in the den.

His father sat where he always did, in a reclining chair turned toward the TV. The sofa where Jamison sat sagged sadly under his weight.

"Daddy," he said. "Mother is unwell. Her leg isn't healing. I spoke to her doctor. He told her they might be able to put a pin in it, then maybe the bone will fuse. But truthfully the problem is her circulation; her leg is not getting enough blood."

His father looked hard at him as he spoke. Jamison had trouble controlling his face, keeping his chin from trembling. "What they think is they will have to amputate her leg, Daddy. Mother doesn't know about it yet. Her doctor will speak to her tomorrow." He was about to suggest that he and his father should be there when the doctor told his mother. His father cleared his throat.

"I wonder if you could—"

"Anything," Jamison said.

He held out his glass. "Bourbon on the rocks. A splash of water."

Jamison made the drink and went back to the sofa. His father shook his head at something on the TV. "That Gingrich," he said. "What a character."

Later, Jamison sat out on the patio drinking gin and tonic. It was cooler now, summer was ending, though the crickets kept up their clamor. A high breeze rattled the dry poplar leaves, and the air seemed to carry a brewing storm, but as the night wore on it came to nothing, and by two o'clock all was calm. He finished his drink and took a walk down his parents' road, then turned onto the street where his friend Paul had lived when they were twelve and in Little League. He passed Paul's house and turned at the next left. He could have walked this route in his sleep.

He pulled out his phone and dialed Jamie's number. He was surprised when Jamie answered.

"The phone is right by my bed," Jamie said. "I'm on call tonight."

"You won't believe where I am standing," Jamison said. "In front of my old high school."

"Is it the same as you remember?" Jamie said.

"Yes! Exactly the same." He looked at the low brick buildings, the portico that ran between them, and could almost hear the bells. He hadn't been miserable there. "You'd think they would have added another building or something. A different color of paint."

"How is your mother?" Jamie said.

He didn't want to talk about his mother, so he said, "My father is losing—no, correction—has lost his marbles. I don't know why I didn't see it before, but he's always been self-absorbed. I guess I thought he was just getting more so. But no. He is no longer *compos mentis*. I see that now. Clear as a bell."

"Are you drunk?" Jamie said. Jamison could hear the smile in his voice.

"Yes. Very. Deservedly so."

"I'm sorry about your father."

"I'm not. Not yet. One sorry at a time."

Jamison's mother's doctor was almost as old as she was, but he had a couple of younger doctors with him who appeared to agree with everything he said. Jamison held his mother's hand while the doctor spoke to her. His mother looked out the window the whole time, until the doctor took the sheet off her leg and pointed his pen at her blackening big toe. Her instep and ankle were a streaky orange-red. Her leg was brown and the flesh scaly to a few inches below her knee; it looked to Jamison like it was made out of wood. The doctor pressed his thumb against her shin to show how the skin didn't give, and pointed out that the rest of her toes were turning various shades of green.

"Excuse me," Jamison said. He went to the bathroom and retched into the toilet as quietly as he could. When he came out of the bathroom, the doctors were gone.

"I don't blame you," his mother said. "It's an awful sight. It deserves to be taken off."

"No," Jamison said. "I think they should wait and see."

"If they wait I might die. I might die anyway. My heart has grown weak. I knew this was happening. It hasn't come as a shock. They're doing it tomorrow."

"I'll call Cathy," he said.

He wept as he told Catherine, and wept after he hung up, the hopeless, helpless tears of a child. He went back to his parents' house. His father was in the den.

"Jamie!" he said. "Good to see you! What brings you down?"

"Mother's surgery," Jamison said, and left the room.

Catherine came that evening with her latest baby.

"Now, he's the last one, I hope," their mother said. "Adorable as they all are. Jamie is seeing someone new, did you know?"

"He did say something about it," Catherine said. "That's great."

"It *is* great," their mother said with unexpected vehemence. "Everyone should be in love at least once."

Jamison smiled. "You were."

"I was indeed."

Catherine looked from Jamison to their mother. "I've missed something, I can see."

Jamison had a dream that night that his mother was playing the piano. Then Jamie was his mother's doctor. Catherine appeared with a tiny baby who turned into a baseball glove. The next morning, he got up and went to the hospital before the sun had completely risen.

His mother was awake. "Darling, what are you doing here? They're not coming for me for hours."

"Couldn't sleep, funny dreams." He sat down next to her bed. "I wanted to see you off."

THE THREE STAGES OF FAT

I LOOK FOR FAT WOMEN wherever I go. Fat women, and women with unhealthy hair, women whose skin is pimply or pocked—or else women who are so lean as to be repellent, arms like sticks, thighs inches apart, cadaverous heads on stem-like necks, so I can say how frightful I think they look, though that isn't true: I would love to look like a coat hanger and have people wonder if I'm ill. I am ill, in fact; I have a condition that makes me fat, and gives me pimples, and causes my hair to shed like a dog's. It's called Baum-Friezinger Syndrome and most people have never heard of it.

I'd never heard of it until I was told that I have it, and explaining to me well enough that I could make sense when I told my family and friends took the doctor fifteen minutes. Unlike cancer or diabetes, diseases that are notorious and potentially dire, my disorder is not fatal, and it doesn't hurt. *Huh,* they say, mild and disinterested, *so that's why...* Meaning that's why I've suddenly gotten so fat, then they promptly forget that none of this is my fault, which is of course the whole reason I told them.

"Well, I know it's not your fault," my husband Douglas consoles me.

"Now you do," I remind him. "But you didn't always."

"Well, neither did you until you went to the doctor."

"I knew something was medically wrong with me. You thought I was a pig."

"I didn't think you were a *pig*. I thought you might be overeating."

"But I wasn't, was I?" I cross my arms over my zeppelin breasts. I love this fight as much as I hate it: he cannot apologize enough.

He sighs. "No, you weren't. I was wrong. Again, Irene, I am very, very sorry."

But sorry doesn't bring back the reflection of myself that I used to see in the mirror. I never realized how beautiful I was until I wasn't anymore. I frame photographs of pre-Baum-Friezinger me and place them around the house. At night in bed I seek out my hipbones beneath their blanket of flesh, and prod my pillowy torso with the tips of my fingers in a mission to discover my ribs. When I sit at my desk at work, my stomach rests on my thighs.

"Isn't there anything you can do?" I beg the doctor.

He looks at me sharply, no pity from him. "There are many worse things than being overweight, Irene."

Of course there are, I know that, I could be in chronic pain or slowly dying; I could be addicted to meth, or homeless, or a quadriplegic with PTSD—I could have been born like this and never have enjoyed twenty-six years of obvious facial bone structure.

He tells me that if I want to have babies, I better get cracking, because Baum-Friezinger can cause infertility.

"But I'm not ready," I say. I'm not! And neither is Douglas, as far as I know—we haven't actually discussed it. Fat and pregnant? What does that even look like?

"Then get ready," the doctor says.

I've never been a woman who craves children. I didn't babysit or enjoy playing with dolls. I don't coo over other people's infants. But I don't want to *not* have them, either; I see children vaguely in the mirage that is the future. My ambivalence, my therapist says, stems from the fact that my parents are narcissists and I was never properly "mirrored," so I am, in effect, still a child trying to make sense of myself. If I had a child of my own, he tells me, I would probably resent it. In fact, I resent the child already, the yet-to-be conceived idea.

"Pregnancy is nothing!" my cousin Carla says. "The baby is the hard part." This she says as she diapers her son without even paying attention to what she's doing.

"You don't get it." I look in the mirror over the changing table, and can see a ghost outline of my pre–Baum-Friezinger face within my udder-like cheeks. My once round eyes have narrowed into beady slits, and my nose, which isn't small, is peppered with blackheads begging to be squeezed. I run my hand through my hair and am gifted with four strands. Growing fatter is unthinkable.

"So you're not skinny!" Carla says impatiently. "Most people aren't." She is, though. She's one of those neat little women who wear a size zero and complain that they can't put on weight. The color of her shingled hair is close to mine, brass with umber undertones, except mine has become just undertones, never on my head long enough to catch a ray of sun. I find myself wishing Carla would get something harmless yet disfiguring, like chronic hives, so we could feel unattractive together.

"Imagine suddenly gaining a lot of weight," I say. "Seriously, put down the baby and really envision yourself thirty, forty pounds heavier."

She doesn't put down the baby, but she does close her eyes for a few seconds before they fly open again like a Chuckie doll's. "But what difference does it make?" she says urgently, as if she's come up with a Big Idea. "I mean, you're fat already, what's twenty more pounds? It will hardly be noticeable! If I were you, I'd get pregnant right away."

There's a difference between being called *not skinny* and being called *fat*. Indulging myself in retail solace, I drive to the mall to look at summer dresses, and for fifteen minutes I forget myself as I admire silk and handkerchief linen and a new kind of cotton called *slubby*. There is a sleeveless black shift that is sublime: the neckline is a simple half-moon scoop, and there are three inches of tiny pleats at the knee; a discreet arc of piping accentuates the high waistline; when I look inside, I see that it's lined. It is exactly the kind of dress I have wanted for years but have never been able to find.

"Excuse me," I say to a passing salesclerk. "Do you have this in an eight?" I used to wear a four, but I'm guessing I'm an eight now.

She is carrying an armful of slacks in Easter egg colors, clearly on her way to doing something with them. She stops short and looks at the dress, looks at me, looks at the dress again. The wide gold hoops in her earlobes sway as her head moves. She is an elegant black woman with lizard green eyes, her Nubian head full of glossy extensions.

"That's an Imelda K.," she says.

"Of course," I say, though I didn't actually look at the label.

She hitches up her load of slacks. "Imelda K. only makes contemporary sizes. Ten is the largest."

"That's fine. I need an eight."

She rifles through the dresses with one hand and fishes out an eight I hadn't seen. I go to the mirror and hold it up against me. My hips overshoot it by about three inches on either side, and the bust barely covers my chest. "I guess I need a ten," I say.

"I don't think so, honey." Again the hoops sway. "I don't see you in a ten. But you might find something similar on three. Plus," she says when I look confused. "The plus sizes are on the third floor."

I feel like I've been punched in the chest. My face is instantly scalding. I have worn a four since I was seventeen. "I'm not a plus!" I say. "I've always shopped on this floor."

"Okay, then let me know if you need help with anything else," she says, and walks away with her load of slacks.

Grabbing a ten, I go to the dressing room, but even before I try it on, I start to cry because I can see it won't fit. I'm miles too wide for this perfect dress. I sit down on the little gold bench and dig through my purse for my phone, but I can't think of one person to call who would make me feel any better. I imagine the clothes on the third floor: flapping floral muumuus and tent-shaped sweaters, bathing suits with skirts. I'm wearing yoga pants that are so tight they're shiny and the stitching at the seams is stressed, and a university sweatshirt that belongs to Douglas, because none of my clothes fit anymore, a fact that I've ignored until now. If you're fat, take my advice and do not look in a three-way mirror. A three-way mirror tells the truth the way no other mirror will.

Douglas is okay with having a baby.

"We were going to have one sooner or later," he says. We're sitting on the sectional in our living room, which I decorated to look like a living room I saw in *House Beautiful*. He's relaxed, sitting with his arms stretched over the back of the couch. He's not the one who has to give birth.

"Do you still find me attractive?" I ask, because conceiving a baby requires sex. I don't know whether it's because the Baum-Friezinger is wreaking havoc on my hormones, or because I think I'm disgusting and assume Douglas does too, but I feel no desire to have sex with him or any other man. We have it, of course, but I could easily not.

"Yes, I do," he says, affronted. "How superficial do you think I am? You're the same person I fell in love with, Irene. I don't care what you look like." But he does, I know he does because *I* care what I look like and I don't even have to look at myself.

"You're lying," I say. "But it's nice of you. If you want to have an affair, I give you permission. Seriously, I would understand."

Douglas is a redhead, and when he gets mad or emotional, the freckles on his face seem to merge. "I don't want to have an affair! What has gotten into you, Irene? Sure, it sucks not to be able to control your weight, but you're going crazy with this Bongfreeger thing—"

"Baum-Friezinger," I say.

"Baum-Friezinger. Are you sure that's the only thing wrong with you?"

"*The only thing wrong with me?*"

"I just mean—"

"Isn't that *enough?* Christ, you're insensitive, Douglas. If you can't understand what I—"

"You're picking a fight with me so we won't have sex," he says. That stops me; I'm really startled. He's absolutely right.

"How can you stand me now?" I say.

"You're not any different now than you were before, Irene."

"Of course I am. I'm not pretty anymore."

He leans forward and clasps his hands between his outspread legs, his elbows resting on his knees. "To tell you the truth, I've never thought you were that pretty."

"What?"

"I mean, you're attractive enough, but what I love is your personality."

I slap his arm playfully. "Stop it." I pick up a framed photo on the side table, a picture of me that Douglas took while we were on vacation in Cancun. I'm striding out of the cerulean sea in a teensy white bikini, water streaming from my taut and tanned body. They are everywhere, these pre-Baum-Friezinger relics. "Why did you take this, then? I look super sexy."

"No, you look happy." He takes the photo from me and admires it, and for a minute I believe him: I am unchanged. That he doesn't think I was pretty is surprising news, but I am strangely not insulted. I feel light, relieved, apart from my body. The late-spring sun streams through the window and brightens Douglas's gingery five o'clock shadow, and the scent of the white lilies I bought this morning and put in a vase is deeply, deliciously sweet. Then Douglas replaces the photo on the side table, and I sink like a submarine.

"I'll never look like that again," I say. I feel like I've been sentenced to die.

Douglas rubs the back of his neck and looks away. "I don't know what else to tell you, Irene. Shit happens, circumstances change. There are worse—"

I leave the room before he can finish.

Maybe I'm already infertile. I make an appointment with my gynecologist, and explain the situation to her.

"Well, let's have a look," she says, rolling a condom onto a penis-shaped probe that attaches to a box that looks like a primitive television. As she slides the thing into my vagina, I realize that I've consented to be defiled by a machine. Dr. Leach is old and very nice, and from a foreign country, but I've never asked which country because her accent sounds German and I'm afraid she'll say Germany, and having a German go at me with a metal implement makes me think of Nazis. I took Douglas's last name, McNulty, when we married, but I am as Jewish as a matzah ball.

Dr. Leach is looking at a static-filled screen that appears to have been swept by a windshield wiper. I see nothing but gray and white fizz, but she says, "There's your right ovary," then moves the penis thing around in me, and says, "And there's the left one!" as if having two is a bonus. She pulls out the penis thing and snaps off its condom. God forbid it should get an STD. "Everything looks fine," she says. "No need to worry. You'll be pregnant before you know it."

I stare up at the acoustic tiles. I am so tired of crying, truly it's exhausting, but nevertheless, tears slide from the corners of my eyes into my ears, which is such an uncomfortable sensation that I have to sit up.

From her low stool, Dr. Leach studies me. The pale, luminescent blue of her eyes reminds me of a husky. "Listen," she says. "There are women who are dying to be pregnant at one end of the scale and at the other end are women who don't want to be at all. In between, the attitudes vary from pleased to reluctant."

"Sure," I say through a stuffed nose.

"But in forty years of practice I have never once seen a woman anywhere on that scale who didn't fall madly in love with her new baby. Sure, there are the diapers and the night feedings, all of that, but what I am telling you is true. No matter how you feel now, you will adore your baby."

I've heard this before, and doubtless she's right, but it doesn't make a mark on my anxiety. I look down at my pink robe, which barely wraps around me, and say, "I don't think I can take any more changes to my body."

She chuckles, which shocks me, given that I am weeping on her examining table. "You can't believe what will happen to your body in time, Irene." She takes my hand and holds it next to hers. Mine is smooth and pale, with shallow whorls at the knuckles. Hers is speckled as a wren's egg, almost more brown than white; the flesh hangs from the bones like crepe, and earthworm-fat veins make tributaries from a hidden fount in her wrist. Her joints are twice the size of mine.

I gasp a little, and she smiles. "I am not a lovely-looking woman. I am old. But do I cry about it? No, of course not! Life is rich. This," she pokes my stomach, "is the card you've been dealt, and you must play it the best you can."

She leaves the room and I get dressed in my plus-size skirt and blouse, avoiding the mirror on the back of the door. Everyone has been talking the same talk, which is, essentially, "Deal with it," but it seems to me that Dr. Leach is the only one who actually walks the walk. I know nothing about her and suddenly want to. I don't even care if she's German. I carry her wisdom through the waiting room full of women and magazines and pamphlets about HPV, and into the dim, wood-paneled elevator, and out onto the midday sidewalk, where the sun is so bright I close my eyes. I stand there, feeling its warmth buffered by a cooling breeze, and think, *Yes, life is rich.*

"Move it, pig." A man bumps past me, causing me to drop my purse.

"Fuck off!" I scream after him as he rushes away, a thing I've never done in my life.

My therapist looks like an actor in a Cialis commercial: middle-aged but still hot. His sandy hair is shot with gray, and there are crinkles around his eyes when he smiles; his teeth have obviously been bleached; he has the body of a triathlete. He wears a business suit, which I appreciate. I used to have a therapist, a woman, who wore denim jumpsuits and Bermuda shorts, and leggings with bold tunics that were too short to hide her ass. I thought her outfits were distracting and unprofessional, so I told her I was moving to

London. I much prefer Dr. Hoff, even if he is a man. His couch is comfortable, too. He assures me that I'm not demented for screaming at a stranger in the street.

"I'm glad to hear it, in fact. You were in denial at first, but now you're angry. The next step is acceptance." He holds up three fingers. "Three stages. I think you're doing very well."

"I *am* angry," I say. "How dare that man call me a pig! I am a human being."

"Yes, you are!" Dr. Hoff says, which makes me think of President Obama's slogan, Yes We Can, which then makes me think of Michelle Obama's incredibly buff upper arms.

"Michelle Obama would be disgusted by me," I say. Dr. Hoff looks puzzled. "But then, if she knew I have Baum-Friezinger she would understand and admire me for being so brave. Because I *am* brave," I nearly shout. "My life has been turned upside down! Nobody understands what's going on with me, but I don't care because I know who I am and what I'm made of..." I trail off because I can't find anything else to say, my thoughts are scrambled wires.

"I understand what's going on with you, Irene. What you are experiencing is known as body dismorphia. You believe you are unworthy because of your appearance, and you are obsessed to the point where you think about it all the time."

"Exactly!" I say. This man is a genius. I was sitting on the couch, but now I lie down. My relief is so profound I feel like dozing.

"But we are going to get you through this," he says.

"Through this to where?"

He holds up three fingers again and says, "Denial, anger, acceptance."

The three stages of fat, I think. "But I don't want to accept it," I say into a tweedy pillow.

"Of course you don't. Not now. You want to be angry about it."

I sit up again. "I think I want to start a foundation or an association or something like that for people with Baum-Friezinger."

"Terrific idea," he says, which makes me feel exactly the way I do when I order at a restaurant and the waiter says Excellent choice.

I know the waiter is just saying that to make me feel good, but I do feel good regardless of knowing that. Dr. Hoff doesn't believe I'm going to start a Baum-Friezinger association any more than I do—I'm already bored with the idea—but I pay him to support me, and support me he does. "You know what, though? I bet if you did a little research you would find that there is already a group of some kind that you might want to join, or do volunteer work for. Channel that anger, Irene."

By the end of the session I am all fired up. I go back to my office and google *Baum-Friezinger foundation*, while eating a salad at my desk. There is no such thing, but there is an online chat group, so I join it under the handle "AngryIrene," and read a few of the posts.

Hi everyone! Imbeauteous here. Does anyone know where I can order one hundred percent cotton T-shirts in size 24? The only T-shirts I can find are polyester blends ☹.

Imbeauteous, try Plusselections.com, they have really nice things. But beware, they're expensive!

Will do. Thanks Chucksmom! ☺

I scan the page and see that it's all pretty much the same, tips on clothing and skins and hair care, and a lot of advice about getting pregnant.

DH and I have been trying for a year now. WTF?

See a specialist ASAP!

I'm on my second IVF cycle, fingers crossed!

Good luck, Grinninggyrl! IUI next week for me. ☺

Suddenly, I feel as if I've run around the block: my heart is pounding and I can't catch my breath. I put my head between my legs, but that doesn't help, so I stagger out into the hallway where Denise, my assistant, sits in her cube. "I can't breathe," I gasp, and she says, "Oh my God!" and that's the last thing I remember before I wake up on the floor.

My co-workers insist on calling an ambulance, and as I lie on the gurney feeling like an idiot, I hear the EMT telling the hospital what to expect through her radio.

"Caucasian female, twenty-six years old, complains of shortness of breath. Otherwise asymptomatic, vitals are normal. She says she has Baum-Friezinger Syndrome."

"I'm not just *saying* it," I say. "It's the truth."

"Not doubting you, ma'am," she says.

I don't think I'm old enough to be called *ma'am*. "And I don't have shortness of breath anymore."

She looks at me, or rather the general area of me, with expressionless eyes. Not only do I feel like I haven't spoken, I feel like I'm not here.

At the hospital I'm startled to be whizzed into the emergency room and immediately seen by a doctor. She's East Indian, dark-skinned and beautiful; her hair is gathered into a huge black bun at her neck. With long, delicate fingers, she holds a stethoscope to my chest, while an automatic blood pressure cuff inhales around my arm.

"My vitals are normal," I say.

"Indeed they are," she agrees and hangs the stethoscope around her neck. "So, tell me, Irene, what happened."

"I don't know, I was in my office and suddenly I felt like I couldn't breathe, then I stood up and I guess I fainted."

"What were you doing when this shortness of breath came on?"

"Looking at my computer." She seems a little impatient, and I find I want to please her. "I was looking at posts in a chat room for women with Baum-Friezinger Syndrome, and it was bumming me out."

"Why, were they sad posts?" she says, frowning to denote sadness.

"No, they were innocuous. Just chat."

"And that upset you."

"Well, I have Baum-Friezinger."

"So I see on your chart."

"That's why I'm so overweight."

"Yes, that's the primary symptom, but you aren't *so* overweight." Her dark eyes sparkle; her smile is brilliant. I love her. "You've been newly diagnosed?"

I nod. "These women... They seemed, you know, okay with it, and it pissed me off. *They* should be pissed off. They should be talking about a cure! I was expecting something more reactionary."

"There is no cure for Baum-Friezinger," she says shortly. She pulls a prescription pad out of her jacket pocket and writes something on it. She tears off the page and hands it to me. "You had an anxiety attack, Irene. This is a prescription for a mild sedative, which you should take as needed. See your physician for a refill." She clicks the pen and pops it into her chest pocket. "You need to chill out." She gives me a kind smile, and walks away just like that.

Denise is waiting for me outside the emergency room.

"I'm fine," I say before she asks. I really wish she'd go away.

"But why did you faint?"

"An anaphylactic reaction to the bok choy in my salad. Who knew? I'll never eat *that* again."

"I called Douglas, he should be here any minute." She is proud that she thought to do this. She is only twenty-one and has a fuzz of down on her cheeks like a chick.

"Denise, do you think I'm fat?"

She raises her eyebrows. I'm her boss, not her friend. "No, not so much. You're a lot bigger than you used to be, but you used to be too skinny. I thought you had an eating disorder when I first met you. I mean, you're so tall and you were, like, this wide." She holds her hands about a foot apart. "That's what everyone thought, actually, that you were kind of anorexic."

"They did?" I'm shocked. "What do they think now?"

She shrugs. "I don't know. That you're not? I mean, people don't really talk about you." She seems embarrassed to admit this. "Well, they do, but only about work things, like, 'Has Irene signed off on that media plan?' Like that."

Why had I assumed the halls were buzzing? Why would they be? Other people's problems are as interesting as other people's pets.

"Do you mind if I ask why you're asking all this?" Denise says.

"Because I am massively self-absorbed," I say. She laughs, and I smile. It's nice that she thinks I'm joking.

Douglas comes and gets me, and we go home and have sex. He's delighted, and so, amazingly, am I. It's the middle of a workday, which is kinky for us. The windows are full of sun, and we're sweating because the central air won't come on until five.

"I'm not using birth control," I tell him after we're done. It's been a while, so we didn't take very long.

"No shit?" He is honestly surprised.

"Throwing caution to the wind."

"You go, girl," he says, and gives me a high five. He runs his fingers through his already crazy hair and gets up to go to the bathroom. I sit up and look at myself in the mirror across the room. The way my breasts loll comfortably on my stomach makes me think of the Venus of Willendorf.

"I'll always look like this," I say when he returns from the bathroom.

He mocks my seriousness. "Yes, I know."

I turn back to the mirror and do something weird: I raise my hand and wave.

"Hello there, me," I say to myself, as if we are meeting for the first time.

ACKNOWLEDGEMENTS

Grateful acknowledgement is made to the publications in which these stories first appeared: "The Truth About Me" in *Cold Mountain Review*, "Vacationland" in *Day One*, "Anything Can Happen" in *Labletter*, "Myrna Athena" in *Corium*, "Mrs Temple" in *The Louisville Review*, "Poor Bob" in *Slippery Elm*, "The Narrow Rim" in *Reed*, "Indoor Voice" as "Crazy Talk" in *The Lascaux Review Prize Anthology*, "Stick Shift" in *Necessary Fiction*, "The Other Rachel Hersch" in *Bayou Magazine*, "What Brings You Down" in *Prime Number*, and "The Three Stages of Fat," in *The Cossack Review*.

Many thanks to April D. Nauman, my first reader and partner in prose, without whom many of the stories in this collection might have withered on the vine. Louise Bruce, Chris Cander, Joni Danaher, Kathi Danaher, Sandi Feldman, Abigail Hastings, Mickey Hawley, Teresa Hudson, William Irvine, Judi Kupermann, Nancy Nygard, David Schweizer, and Mary Volmer have been valued readers and supporters. I am profoundly grateful to everyone at the Sewanee Writers Conference. WTAW Press and Peg Alford Pursell, thank you with all my heart for ushering this book into the world. I am deeply in debt to my husband, Charles Marburg, for reading multiple drafts of every story I've written.

About the Author

Louise Marburg attended the Kansas City Art Institute, is a graduate of New York University, and holds an MFA in Fiction from Columbia University's School of the Arts. She lives in New York City and Connecticut with her husband, the artist Charles Marburg. For more information, visit her online at louisemarburg.com.

WTAW Press is a 501 (c) 3 nonprofit press and thanks the
following supporters for their assistance.

Anonymous	Molly Giles	Cheryl Morris
Maria Benet	Mark Goldrosen	Ginger Murchison
Rosaleen Bertolino	Gary Hawkins	John Phillip
Amanda Conran	Patrick Hayes	Anne Raeff
Walter B. Doll	Dorothy Hearst	Marleen Roggow
Audrey Ferber	Mary Herr	Aran Ramsey Tate
Charlene Finn	Leslie Ingham	Anne Taylor
DB Finnegan	Susan Ito	Elizabeth Terzakis
Gerald Fleming	Scott Landers	Janet Thornburg
Rebecca Foust	Richard May	Debra Turner
Joan Frank	Denise Miller	Townsend Walker
Stephanie Fuelling	Alison Moore	Olga Zilberbourg